I0611778

My Alien Visitors

Extended Edition

Stan Shabronsky

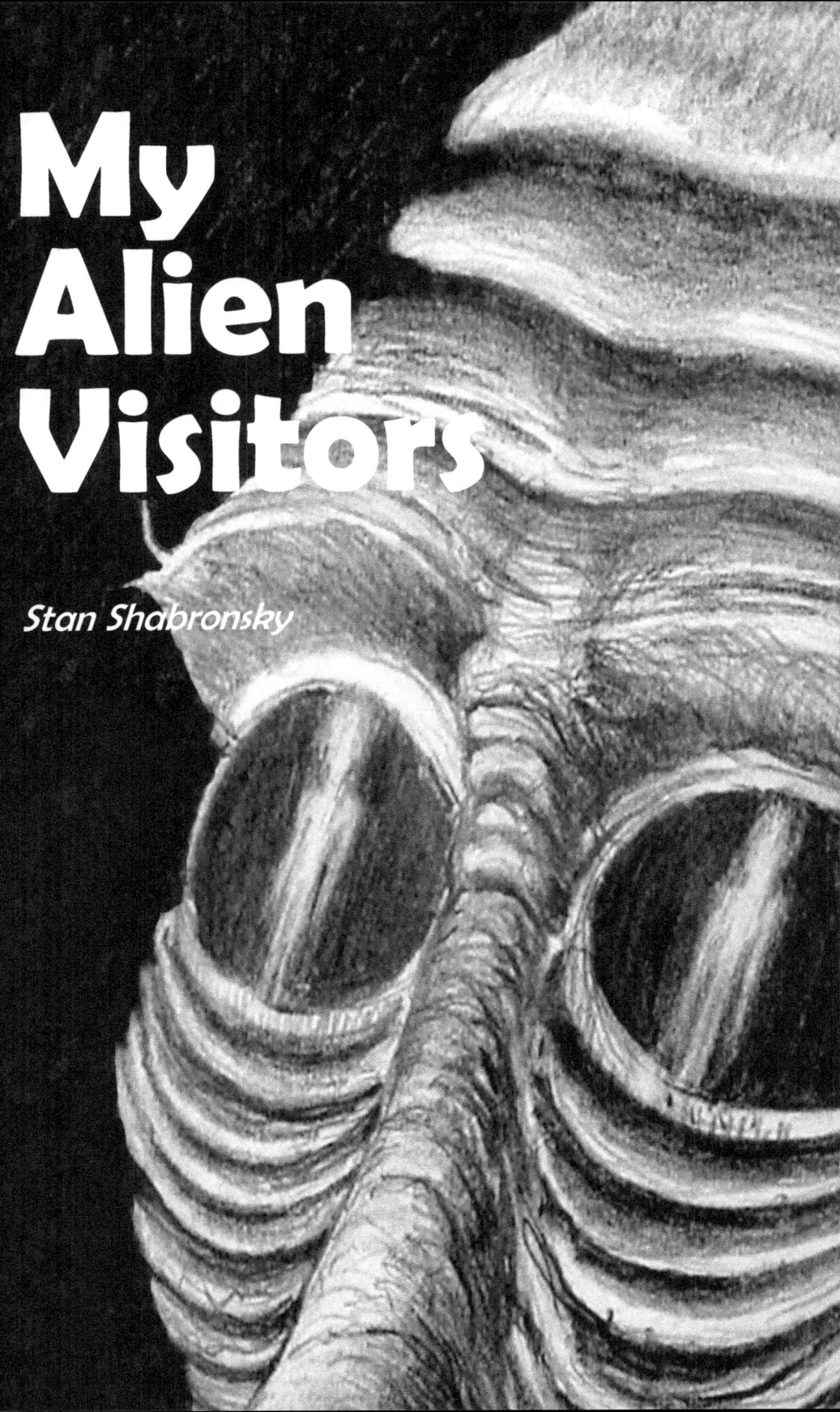

My Alien Visitors

Stan Shabronsky

I see what she
means other Worldly-ness ! How did you draw
these? With conte crayon,pencil?t How large is it ?
... *doggy paddler*

HI PEOPLE
I HAVE 2 ALIEN GUESTS OVER FOR
THE WEEKEND.
HIS NAME IS MORRIS, THE OTHER ONE
.(IN THE BACKGROUND)
IS MANDY, SHE DOESN'T TALK VERY MUCH.
A BIT WIERD I THINK, BUT SHE WILL
EVENTUALLY BE AT EASE WITH ME.
I DON'T KNOW WHY I'M GETTING VISITORS
SOMEHOW WORD GOT OUT THAT I DRAW
ALIEN PORTRAITS AND THAT GIVES THEM THE
EXCUSE TO VISIT ME AND MAKE CONTACT
WITH ME. SINCE I KNOW THAT THEY
ARE VERY AFRAID OF CAMERAS AND
AVOID BEING PHOTOGRAPHED. THEY
DON'T TRUST ANYTHING THAT'S AIMED OR
POINTED AT THEM,THIS THEN BECAME A
WONDERFUL OPPORTUNITY FOR ME
....STAN

"OH! WOW That is awesome Stan !!
I love the composition, like Carravagio in your face!
Then There is the faint image in the background,
Great contrast. Kudos"
... *Picasso53*

Morris

OK PEOPLE HERE SHE IS. THE GAL THAT WAS HIDING
BEHIND MORRIS. NOW OUT OF THE SHADOWS INTO
THE SUNLIGHT, AND THE FIRST THING SHE DOES...IS
ORDER A SET OF PEARLS VIA: COMPUTER ON-LINE
SHOPPING AND SHE'S OUT TO PAINT THE TOWN GREEN.
BEING A GIRL FRIEND OF MORRIS SHE WAS
ORIGINALLY CLONED AND TRANSPORTED TO THE
MORRIS HOMESTEAD, TO IMPROVE
THE TAPLINE BREED OF FUTURE GENERATIONS.
APPARENTLY WHAT HAPPENED, WAS THAT MORRIS'
BLOOD CHEMISTRY DNA WAS ALTERED, WHEN HE
VENTURED OUT OF THE SOLAR SYSTEM TO SEEK
OUT NEW HORIZONS, WHERE NO ONE HAS GONE
BEFORE. SO THE LAB GUYS CAME UP WITH
THIS GAL. SHE'S A BIT SHY. ALTHOUGH MORRIS
LOOKS MEAN, HE'S REALLY A GENTLE CREATURE
THEY SHOULD GET ALONG WELL WITH THE
"SEED-EGGS" FROM THIS UNION AND SHOULD BE
BENEFICIAL TO ALL ALIEN-KIND.

IT SHOULD BE EXPLAINED; THAT MOST
ALIENS DO NOT GIVE BIRTH TO BABIES . THEY
BIRTH TO WHAT IS CALLED A "SEEDEGG"
HATCHED BY THE MOM, AND CARED
FOR BY MOM, DAD OR ANYONE OR ANY PERSON . I WAS
GIVEN THIS HONOR ... IT'S
CALLED AN "SEED-EGG" BECAUSE OF ITS
UNLIMITED TIME ON WHEN IT COULD
HATCH; HOURS, DAYS, MONTHS, OR DECADES LATER.

MANDY

Plantoid

THIS WAS A SPECIAL "SEED-EGG," DELIVERY
FROM AN ALIEN VISITOR. IT CAME WITH
INSTRUCTIONS
ON HOW TO PLANT IT IN THE GARDEN.
THE ORIGINAL MULTI—HEADED
" **PLANTOID 1** " WERE ALIEN PROTECTORS.
THEY
ACHIEVED A HEIGHT OF 15 FEET AND
A GRASPING DISTANCE OF 30', ,,, FOR ACTIONS
AGAINST AN ENEMY ALIEN ATTACK OF
INVADING GIANT
WASPS, ON IT'S OWN HOME PLANET. HOWEVER
FOR EARTH USE, A DOMESTIC VARIETY
" **PLANTOID 2** ," WAS DEVELOPED, AS
SHOWN IN THE
ILLUSTRATION, AS IT IS BEING
SELECTIVE, IN IT'S OFFENSIVE ACTION. IT
WOULD SNARE-HOOK ALL
INSECTS EXCEPT OF COURSE BUTTERFLIES, BEES,
SPIDERS AND DRAGONFLYS. RIGHT NOW AS
YOU CAN SEE, SHE'S PLAYING WITH A NEW
FOUND PLAYMATE. THIS ONE WILL ONLY GROW TO
ABOUT 3 FEET .
THIS IS A ROOTED CREATURE AND SINCE IT
HIBERNATES IN WINTER,
A PROTECTIVE WEATHER COVER IS REQUIRED.

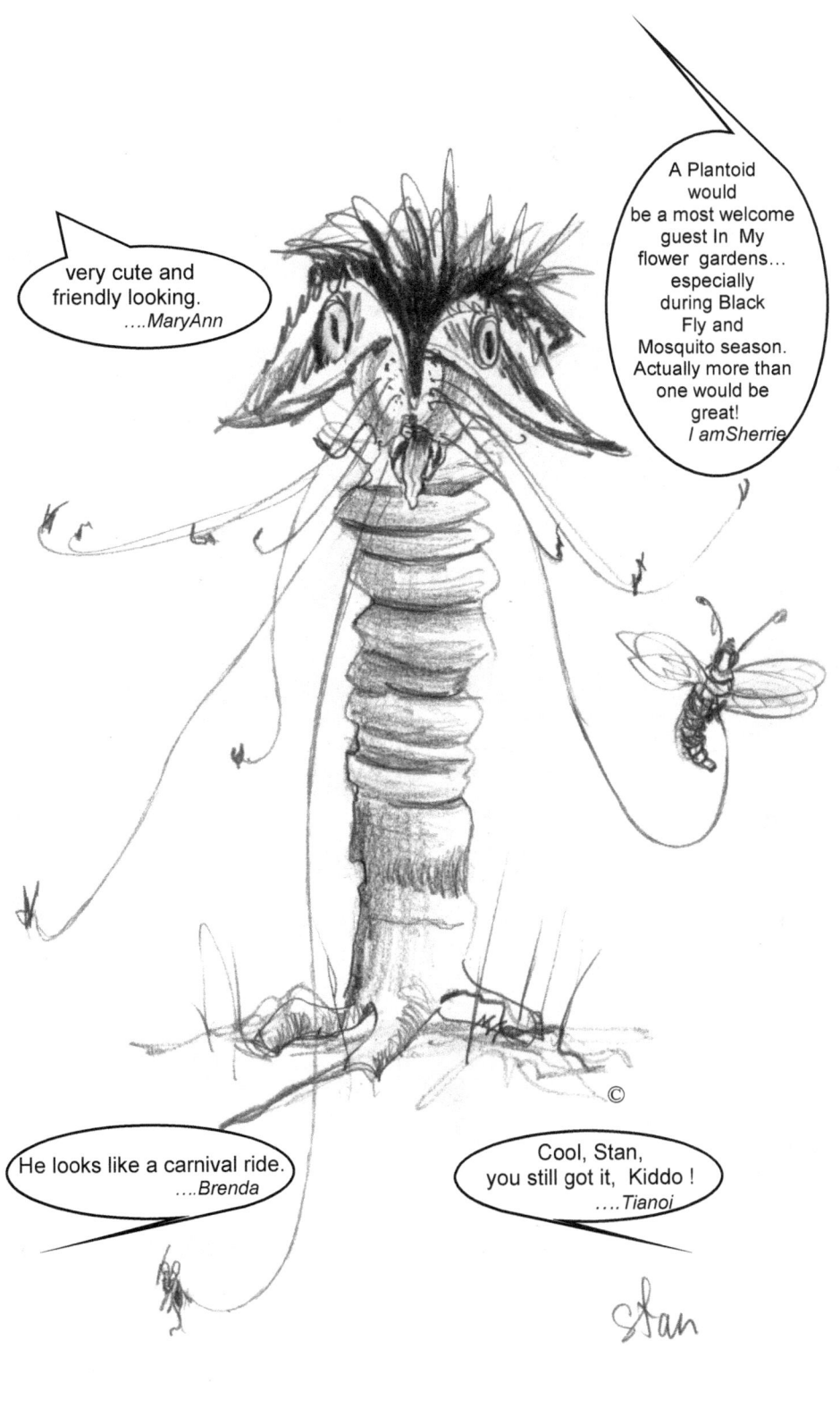

WITH ALL THIS TALK ABOUT ALIENS,
IS THE STUFF THAT IMAGINATION IS
MADE OF,
IT'S MY THEORY THAT
" FUTURE ALIENS" HAVEN'T LEFT EARTH
YET. SPECIFIC CONDITIONS MUST FIRST
TAKE PLACE. LIKE FINDING A PLANET
"CLOSE ENOUGH " TO EARTH'S
SIMILARITIES, FOR BASIC HUMAN
NEEDS AND SURVIVAL.
THAT ORIGINAL DIFFERENCE WOULD BE
ENOUGH TO PRODUCE GENETIC CHANGES.
AFTER SEVERAL MILLION YEARS
LATER WE WILL HAVE THE
"FUTURE ALIEN."
IT WILL BE DIFFERENT FROM THE PRESENT
EARTH DWELLERS. IF WE HUMANS ARE
STILL AROUND TO WITNESS AND GREET THE
VISITING ALIENS. IN THE MEANTIME SAY
HELLO TO MATTHEW,
A 10 YEAR OLD, "SEED-EGG " CHILD OF
MANDY AND MORRIS.

Matthew:

" I do not Question or comment on Aliens However, he looks like me, thinks like me ,He could be my father. I see a Strong resemblance. I think this alien is one of us, Wearing a mask. Keep up the good job Peace Profound.". ..Albert Depas
......."and he is an excellent and keen observer. Nothing happens without him noticing . He would make an excellent school teacher " .....pucipaci
"Weird, Stan"" Vision375
©
"That's a whole lotta eyes!" ...Dipsydue2
"Nice I Like the human characteristics" ..Potterlgrl

HEY GUESS WHAT ?
THIS LITTLE CUTIE
BUMPS AGAINST MY DOOR EARLY THIS
MORNING..., LOOKING UP AT
ME WITH HER BIG DARK EYES .
WAS ORIGINALLY DELIVERED TO ME AS
A SEED-EGG SOMEHOW WORD GOT OUT
THAT I'M AN ARTIST AND SHE
BEING FULLY GROWN
FEET HIGH, SHE WANTED ME TO DRAW
HER, SO HOW COULD I SAY NO ?
AS YOU SEE DEBBIE IS
BONDING WITH THE FIRST THING THAT
LANDED ON HER.
SHE'S PLAYING WITH IT, ON THE
TIP OF HER TONGUE ... SHE
WILL EAT OTHER INSECTS, BUT
NOT THIS ONE.
THEY ARE FRIENDS FOREVER.

I think that you should put a
shrink on a yearly retainer!! Don't worry he
will never take you away with the net. They may take away
the thing on her tongue, its an endangered species.
Actually so are you******
... Howie R.

"He looks good, more human "
...Frank

HI PEOPLE I'M BACK.
I HAD A GUEST FROM THE PAST,
IT WAS MY OLD FRIEND NARLO, BEFORE
HE WAS PROMOTED TO CAPTAIN OF A
SPACE SHIP.
HE WAS TRYING TO FIND A MORE
ENVIRONMENTALLLY SAFE PLANET.
WHEN THE SHIP WAS CAPTURED.
THE PASSENGERS WERE THEN BEING
TRANSPORTED TO AN ALIEN MUSEUM
PRISON FOR VISUAL DISPLAY AND
AMUSEMENTFOR THEIR
CAPTORS. HOWEVER THEIR CAPTAIN
HAD AN ESCAPE PLAN,
UNDER COVER OF A MOONLESS NIGHT,
HE MANAGED TO USE THE SPACE SHIP
WHICH HE CALLED THE ARK, AS AN
ESCAPE ROCKET SHIP TO FREE ITSLF OF
THE ALIEN PLANET.

MY FRIEND NARLO AND STELLA THEN
AGREED TO
AN INFORMAL PORTRAIT, AS YOU
WILL SEE IN THIS AND THE NEXT PAGE
...STAN

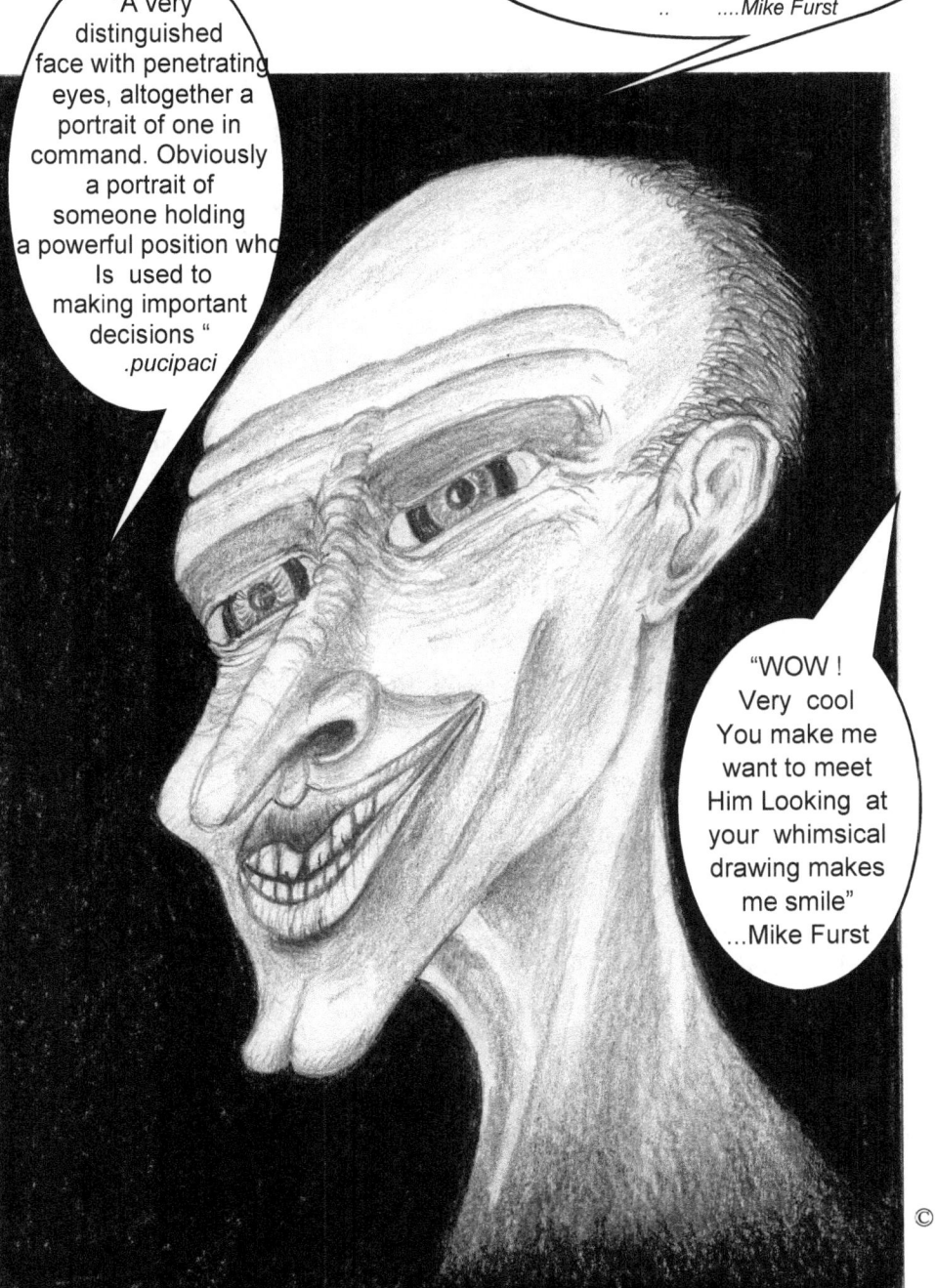

OK PEOPLE HERE SHE IS
STELLA
GIRL FRIEND OF CAPT. NARLO, COMMANDER OF THE
SPACE SHIP "ARK" YOU'VE HEARD SO MUCH ABOUT.
SHE FINALLY STOPPED OVER, WE HAD A
NICE FRIENDLY CHAT. A VERY TALL GAL, AT LEAST
7 FEET TALL AND
I NOTICED HER AMAZING EAR HANGINGS ..
I FIRST REMARKED, HOW BEAUTIFUL ARE THOSE
STAR HANGINGS .
"THOSE STAR HANGINGS "? SHE REMARKED
IT'S JUST TWO INVERTED OVERLAPPING TRIANGLES.

WE DID TALK ABOUT OUR FAMILES ...WHEN STELLA
FIRST SPOTTED MY MALTESE HOUSE PET,
SHE BECAME HORRIFIED...REMARKING HOW
CAN I LIVE WITH SOMETHING SO UGLY? ..WELL I SAID,
"THE WIFE LIKES IT ",
SHE UNDERSTOOD. ANYWAY AFTER SEVERAL
HOURS OF TALKING, SHE CONFRONTS ME WITH THIS..
" I'M HEAVY WITH
SEED-EGG AND I MUST STAY OVERNIGHT.
TO LAY IT IN YOUR HOUSE " ..I SAID; WHAT ! ..HOLD ON !
" NOT TO WORRY." SHE REPLIED " THE SEED- EGG
WILL EASILY HATCH, A BRIGHT LIGHT FOR FEW HOURS
EACH DAY, IS ALL THAT IS REQUIRED.
THE EGG WILL HATCH AND TAKE CARE OF ITSELF.
.I SAID , WAIT ! .. WHAT ABOUT CARE, FEEDING ?
HOW CAN I DO THIS ?
SHE SAID, " IT'LL FEED ITSELF... JUST OPEN A CAN OF
DOG FOOD . I'VE ALREADY RESEARCHED THIS, IT'S
GOOD FOOD" . ..I THOUGHT ABOUT THAT, .
NEVER ARGUE WITH A
WOMEN, ESPECIALLY AN ALIEN GAL.

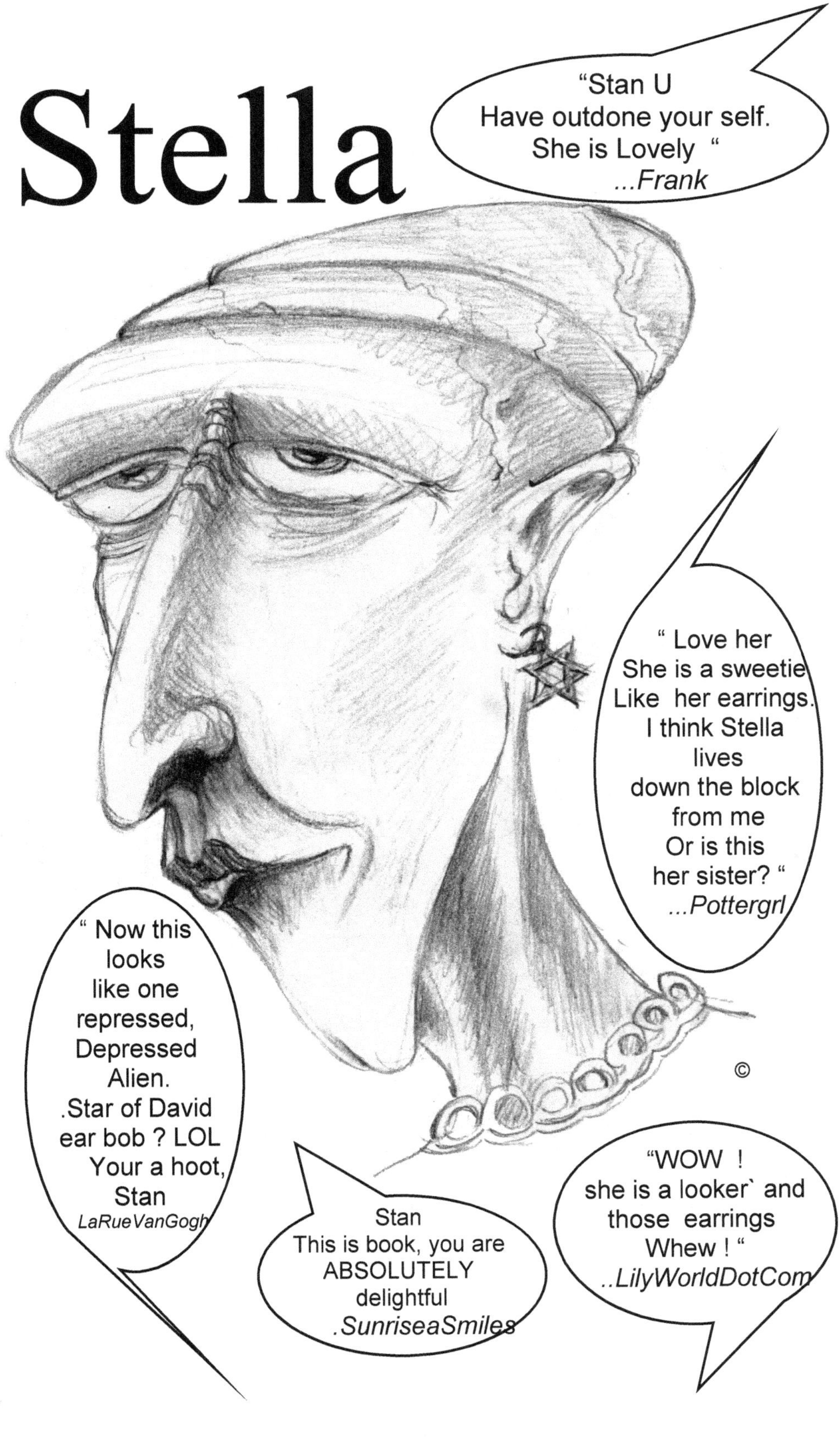

BRACiPALiA

EVERYONE STAY CALM.
THIS IS JUST A BRACiPALiA
WHICH IS NOTHING MORE THAN AN EFFICIENT
HOUSE PEST ELIMINATOR. NOW ONLY AVAILABLE
THROUGH CLONING.
THEY ARE APPROXIMATELY 75 TO 125 MM. IN LENGTH
IT CAN EASILY FIT INTO A LADIES HANDBAG OR
PERCH, ON A MANS SHOULDER, WHILE TRAVELING TO
MOTELS OR HOTELS THAT MIGHT HARBOR
INSECTS. THESE DARLING CREATURES UNLIKE THE
ORIGINAL LARGER SIZES, ARE
LABORATORY CLONED AND CANNOT REPRODUCE.
THERE IS NO COST, FREE TO ALL MEMBERS.
ONCE PLACED IN A DARK ROOM AND WHILE
YOU'R ASLEEP, IT WILL EFFECTIVELY ELIMINATE
ROACHES, BED BUGS FLEAS AND ANTS. PLEASE NOTE,
\WILL NOT HARM SPIDERS. ORDERS RECEIVED BY
THE FIRST OF THE MONTH WILL BE FILLED
WITHIN A FEW DAYS. PLEASE NOTE A BRACiPALiA
ONLY EATS LIVE FOOD, SO YOUR SNACK FOOD LEFT
ON A TABLE WILL NOT BE CONSUMED.
A GREAT GIFT FOR ANY HOME, APARTMENT, MOTEL,HOTEL,
SCHOOL LUNCHROOMS AND PRISON CELLS..
OH YES! BEFORE I FORGET AFTER ITS NIGHT OF
ITS HUNTING. .. YOU MAY WAKE UP WITH IT ON
YOUR PILLOW EXHAUSTED AND SLEEPING.DO NOT
ROLL OVER ON IT, THEIR DEFENSIVE BITES
COULD BE NASTY

OK PEOPLE, MEET SETH.
HE'S WAVING HIS ARMS NOT AS A GREETING
BUT RATHER AS AN INSTINCTIVE PART OF
USING HIS SPIKES TO CRACK OPEN THE
SEED-EGG AND FREE HIMSELF OF EGG
HELL PARTICLES. SETH LEFT THE HIBERNATION
AREA AND IS NOW EATING A CAN OF
DOG FOOD EACH DAY...
THIS IS WHAT STELLA, HIS MOTHER, IN-
STRUCTED ME TO FEED HIM.. ANYWAY I'M GLAD
HIS EGG SPIKES FELL OFF
BELIEVE THIS OR NOT, SETH AND OUR PUP ARE
GETTING ALONG JUST FINE. THE PUP IS NOW
LICKING HIS FACE, WELL...
THERE IS NO ACCOUNT FOR TASTE.
ANYWAY MOM IS READY TO PICK HIM UP IN A
FEW WEEKS. SETH IS ALREADY WALKING ON
HIS OWN..
EVEN MY WIFE REMARKED
"OH MY! HOW QUICKLY THEY GROW"
I HOPE STELLA WILL COME SOON
BECAUSE SETH IS STARTING TO BOND WITH
OUR DOG.
I DID HEAR HIM BARK A FEW TIMES
DURING THE DAY.
OH YES! SETH FINALLY LEARNED HOW TO
THE FLUSH THE TOILET.

Seth

OK GUYS AND GALS WELCOME
IRENE A "DUOPUS"..
NOT IN ANYWAY CONNECTED TO THE OCTOPUS,
AN EIGHT-LEGGED VAGABOND.
THIS GAL IS SOPHISTICATED AND HUMBLE,
WILL RECEIVE ALL VISITORS BUT ONLY ON A
ONE TO ONE BASIS. AN AIR BREATHING GAL
THAT LIKES TO SIT IN A WARM POOL ALL
DAY, ENJOYING THE SUN, WHILE MUNCHING
HER LATEST FAVORITE FOOD, HOT DOGS.
GUESTS HOWEVER CAN BRING THEIR OWN
SNACKS AS WELL, WHILE
SHE'S TALKING ABOUT HER ADVENTURIOUS
SEA LIFE.
SHE ORIGINALLY CAME TO ME AS A
"SEED- EGG"
BY A PREVIOUS ALIEN GUEST, THAT
HATCHED IN MY HOUSE . IRENE'S DNA
CONTAINED ALL THE LIFE EXPERIENCES OF
HER ANCESTORS,
SO OBVIOUSLY THERE WAS NO NEED FOR HER
TO RE-LEARN. AND...DONT BE FOOLED BY
THE FISH SHE'S EATING
..IT'S JUST HER PET FISH .. SHE'S DOING
THAT TO IMPRESS THE TOURISTS.

DUOPUS

Irene

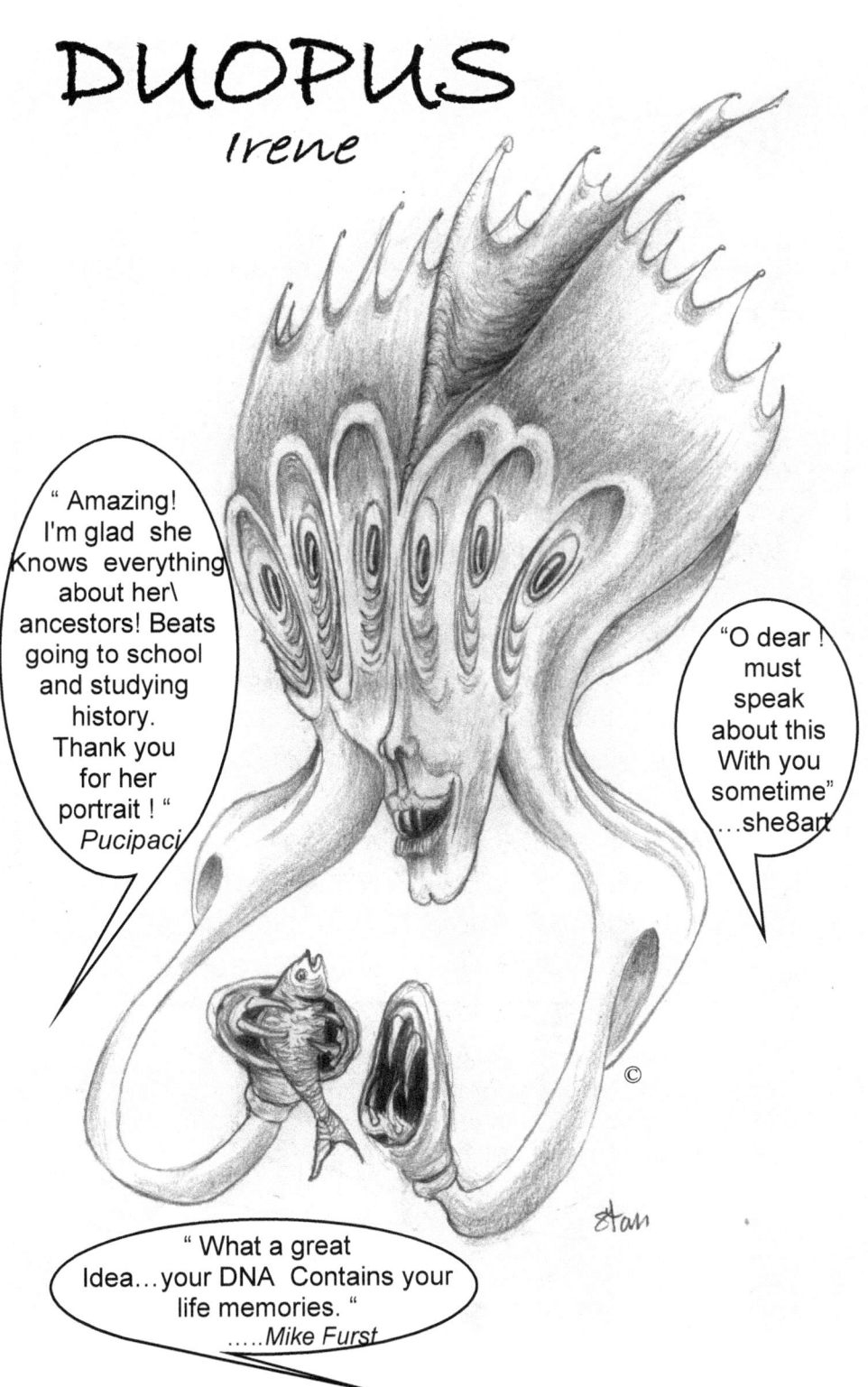

" I'm speechless Nice drawing
tho. His head looks like a pencil Eraser
          "   ...*Ephmera again*

OK PEOPLE, MEET
SETH, THE SON OF CAPT. NARLO & STELLA,
SETH IS ALREADY BUSY USING THE COMPUTER. SETH
APPEARS TO BE A HEALTHY DELIGHTFUL 8 1/2 YR OLD,
IS CAPABLE OF LIVING 500 YRS EARTH TIME. AND
AS MY WIFE RECENTLY REMARKED
" MY! HOW QUICKLY THEY GROW "
THANK GOODNESS HE FINALLY LOST THOSE EGG SPIKES
JUST AFTER HATCHING.. I'VE HEARD OF SITUATIONS
WHERE THEY DON'T FALL OFF, THAT WOULD HAVE
BEEN TERRIBLE ON MY FURNITURE. WE FINALLY
WEANED HIM OFF DOG FOOD AND STARTED HIM EATING
CHICKEN WITH RAW CABBAGE.
HE STILL SLEEPS WITH EGG SHELLS ..MUST BE
SOME SORT OF SECURITY THING. ANYWAY, AS I'M
SENDING THIS NOTICE OUT,
MOM AND SETH ARE STANDING AT THE
DOORWAY ABOUT TO LEAVE, HE TURNS TOWARD US.
WITH A SMILE, AND A TEAR IN HIS EYE HE
WAVED GOOBYE , ANDTHEY WERE GONE.

" I wonder what Seth
would be like when he grows up,
probably very popular with the ladies.
I'm glad you had plenty of dog food for him."
          ...*PuciPaci*

" Genetic variation. Note differences from
parent.They were right in introducing DNA strands in
early humans...One never knows when they
will be expressed (or how) "
          ....*Mike F.*

Seth

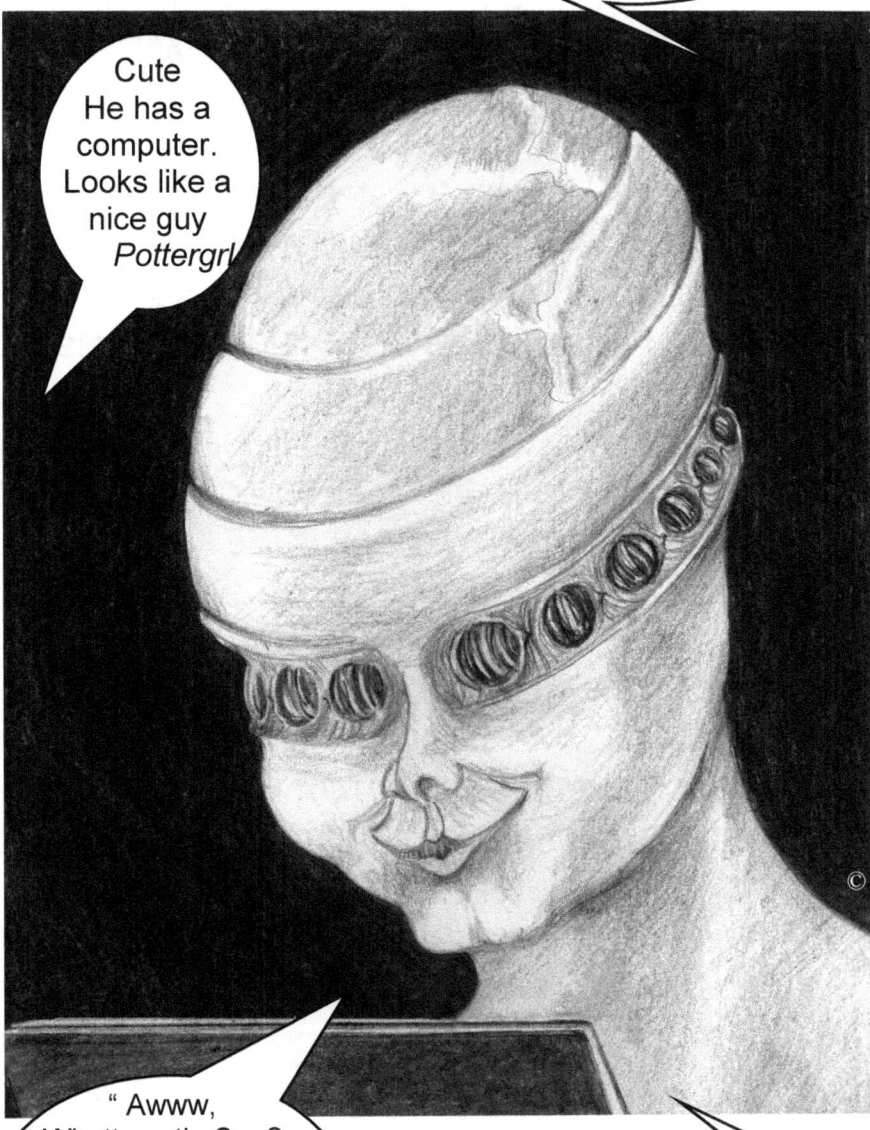

OK PEOPLE HERE'S A FLASH FOR YOU
THE ORIGINAL CLONED GROUP OF THE
IMPORTED EDEX'S, WERE RELEASED EARLY THIS
MORNING AND PROBABLY HEADING FOR
FLORIDA OR VIRGINIA BEACHES. THEY WERE
DESIGNED TO BE DAYTIME
BEACHCOMBERS WHO CRAWL THROUGH WET OR
DRY SAND, HUNTING FOR SEA SHELLS, OYSTERS.
THEY WILL ALSO CLIMB INTO GARBAGE CANS. AT
DUSK THEY'LL SLEEP FURTHER OUT IN THE
WATER UNTIL SUNRISE.
BEACH WALKERS HAVE NO NEED TO WORRY, BUT
IT'S A GOOD IDEA TO CARRY SOME FOOD; NUTS,
POTATO CHIPS...ETC. WITH YOU, AND TOSS IT
TO THEM. THEY ARE VERY FRIENDLY CREATURES,
SOME MAY EVEN FOLLOW YOU TO YOUR CAR.
PLEASE NOTE: AS THEY ARE ENVIRONMENTALLY
PROTECTED, IT'S ILLEGAL TO TAKE THEM HOME
AS PETS. PLEASE DO NOT PHOTOGRAPH THEM, IT
SCARES THEM. THEY DO HOWEVER LIKE TO
POSE FOR A DRAWING, SUCH AS WHAT
YOU SEE HERE.

"EDEX is a winner
so handsome and
loved the story"
...JIM

"These are the stuff
that give nightmares. That means
you are damn good at it. Heh"
…... Mrs3bits

EDEX

OK PEOPLE MEET THIS GROWN-UP FRIEND WE CALL

Kelley

ORIGINALLY OFFERED TO ME AS A GIFT BRANCH CUTTING FROM THE " ●●● " CREATURE. KELLEY USED TO BE A HUMANOID FRIEND OF MINE THAT WAS LOOKING FOR IMMORTALITY. SO AFTER A LENGTHY DISCUSSION, WE DECIDED ON A FULLY MOBILE TREE, WAS THE PERFECT VENUE. TO ACCOMPLISH THIS FEAT IT WOULD SIMPLY BE A MATTER OF TRANSPOSING (OVERLAPPING) ITS DNA WITH THE CARBO-CELLULOSE TREE DNA. THE EXPECTED RESULT WOULD BE THE DEVELOPMENT OF KELLEY INTO AN ACTUAL MOBILE AND ROOTLESS TREE. THE PROCEEDURE WAS COMPLICATED BUT THE G ENETICISTS WERE ABLE TO BE FULLY SUCCESSFUL. SIMPLY PUT, IT'S JUST A WAY OF EXTENDING A HUMANS LIFE INTO A MUCH LONGER LIVING CREATURE, UNLIKE SOME OF OLD HOLLYWOOD'S FICTION SCIENCE "NON-SENSE". MY KELLEY CREATURE IS FOR REAL, AND WILL NOW HAVE A LIFE EXPECTANCY TO OVER 200 YEARS AND WILL HAVE THE CAPABILITY OF EXTENDING ONES LIFE, BY SHIFTING ONES LIFE INTO THE NEWER BRANCH CUTTING. KELLEY WILL BECOME A FULL SIZED WITHIN A MONTH. HOWEVER KELLEY BEING FULL GROWN COULD NOT ENTER OUR DOORWAY . NON THE LESS KELLEY IS ALWAYS INVITED TO HAVE COFFEE AND OAK-MAPLE COOKIES WITH US ON THE BACK PATIO. IN THE EVENING KELLEY WILL STROLL ALONG THE WATERS EDGE..AND WHEN PEOPLE APPROACH, WILL JUST CLOSE ITS EYES, AND REMAIN MOTIONLESS, DISGUISING ITSELF AS A TREE. AND IS NOW HAPPY IN THE NEW LIFETYLE, THE NEW BASIC FOODS ARE INSECTS THAT TRY TO FLY PAST ITS FLEXIBLE LIMBS, AND WITH TREE RESTING BIRD FRIENDS, THAT WILL MAKE KELLEY SMILE.

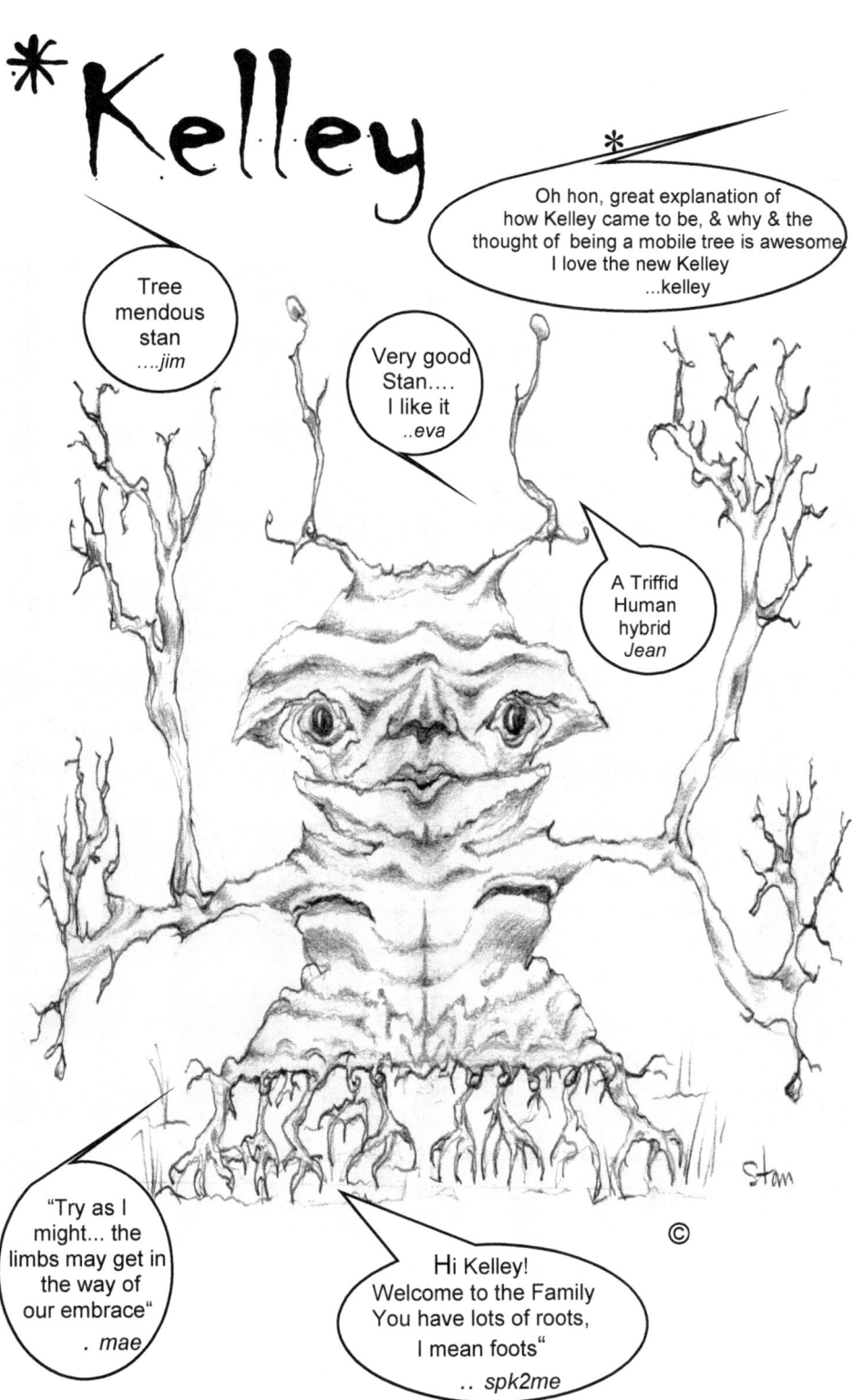

THIS "SEED-EGG" HATCHED AND I
HAD PROBLEMS WITH THIS CREATURE. IT
DEMANDED TO BE RELEASED, SO UNDER THE
COVER OF DARKNESS I SET IT
FREE ON THE NEAREST PUBLIC BEACH. IT'S
JUST THAT IT GOT BORED WITH DOG FOOD, AND
STOPPED EATING. IT REALLY LIKES EASY
SNACKING JELLYFISH; AND HAS NO KNOWN
ENEMIES, SEAGULLS WON'T GO NEAR THIS ONE.
IN ITS DEFENSE IT CAN EAT OR
BORE ITS WAY OUT OF A SHARK'S STOMACH.
THE ONLY SEA CREATURE IT CAN MAKE FRIENDS
WITH, IS THE SEA TURTLE. AND   SINCE THE
AQUA -CROCODIPOD HAS NO FLIPPERS. THEY HAVE
BEEN KNOWN TO ATTACH ITSELF TO SEA
TURTLES, IT WILL THEN BOND AND PROTECT IT.
DURING ITS SEA WANDERINGS

" Must have interesting
metabolism since it can go without air as
long as a sea turtle. Exoskeleton construction means
that it must shed and at times be like a 'soft shell'
crab Nothing like that here on earth "-
… Mike

" Looks like a little
sea demon Stan "
.....LilyWorldDotCom

Aqua-Crocodipod

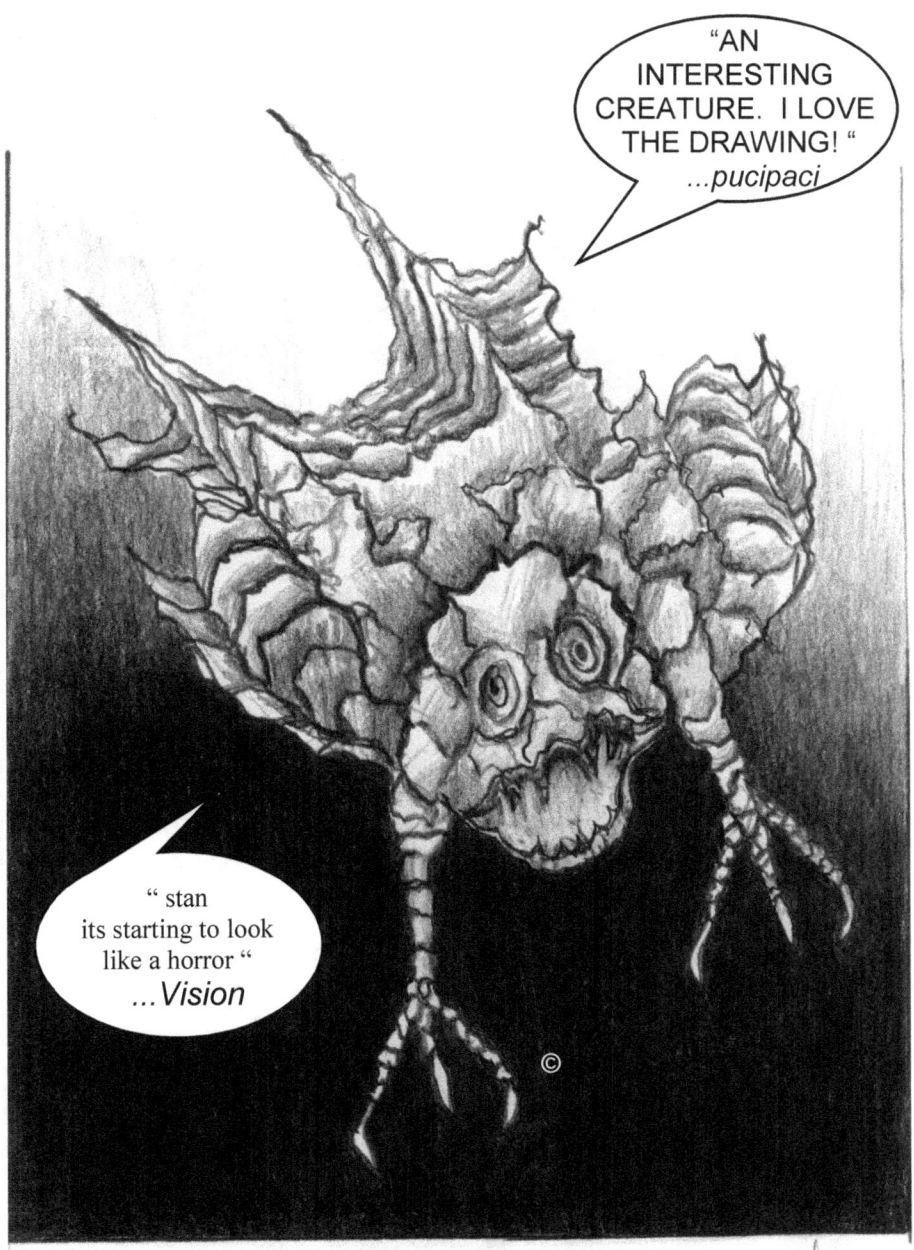

ARNAT

A SOPHISTICATED ALIEN LADY WITH A ROYAL EGYPTIAN BLOODLINE. I MET HER AND FAMILY SOME TIME AGO
WHAT I UNDERSTAND IS THAT HER ANCESTORS VENTURED TO EARTH, SOME 8000 YRS AGO. AND LIVED WITH EGYPTIAN FAMILIES, AFTER SOME 2500 YRS LATER
SOME OF THE FAMILY TRANSPORTED BACK TO THEIR HOME PLANET. DURING THAT TIME NATURALLY SOME DNA AND GENETIC CHANGES TOOK PLACE.

AS OF NOW SHE'S TOGETHER WITH SETH, YOU REMEMBER SETH ? THATS THE LAD, WHO GREW UP IN MY HOME, YEARS AGO.. WHO IS THE SON OF CAPT. NARLO AND STELLA. BOTH ARNAT AND SETH MET DURING A SOCIAL GATHERING AT
AN UNDISCLOSED LOCATION RIGHT HERE ON EARTH, TO WHERE I WAS INVITED AND AFTER TALKING, THEY BOTH AGREED THAT I WOULD BE WATCHING OVER THEIR FIRST "SEED-EGG"
WHENEVER THEY ARE READY.

ARNAT

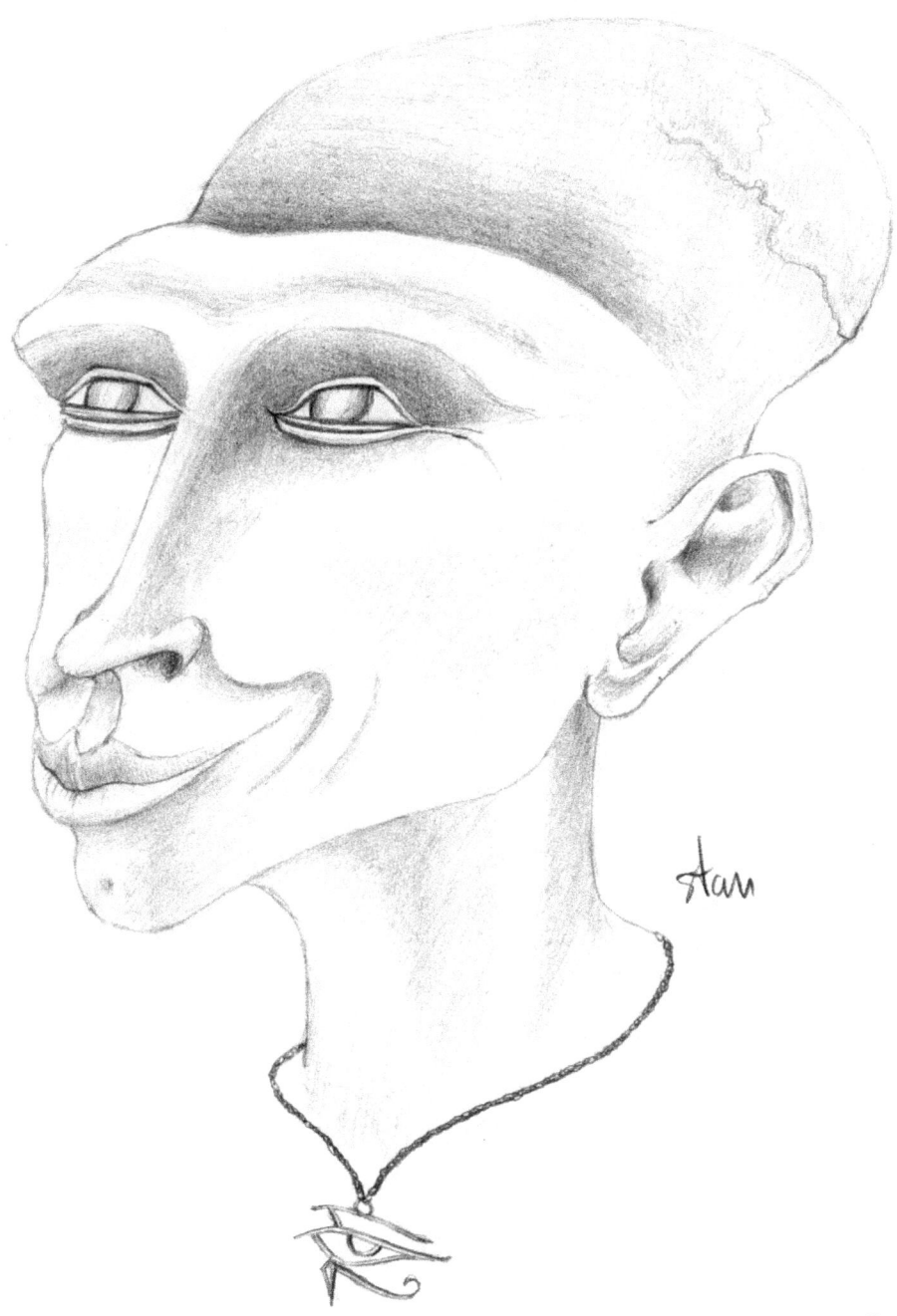

" I do not think I want to be a
butterfly at this moment. Just doesn't
seem safe now. Thank you for the warning
AH! I forgot, I'm a human "
...*PuciPaci*

NOW WHAT ?
SOMEBODY IN THE LABORATORY ERRED ON
THE CARBO-PROTEIN MIX DURING THE
CREATION OF A WASP HUNTER, A
TRIMADIPOD.
APPARENTLY IT WAS ACCIDENTLY RELEASED
NEAR THE N.Y. BROOKLYN BOTANICAL GARDENS.
E INTERNAL STRUCTURE CONTAINED A CODED
DNA INSTINCT BIO PLATFORM, WHICH WAS
ACCIDENTALLY ALTERED ..CREATING A
BUTTERFLY PREDATOR; WHICH IS TOTALLY
ILLEGAL.. WE ARE CURRENTLY IN THE
PROCESS OF DESIGNING A GEL MIX, WITH A
HIGH FLAG RECALL RATE . THAT
SHOULD LURE IT BACK TO THE LABS. IF THERE
ARE ANY PEOPLE WHO HAVE SUGGESTIONS AS
WELL AS THOSE WILLING TO APPLY THIS GEL TO
THE SIDES OF CELL PHONE TOWERS, FENCE
POSTS, BUILDING CORNERS, FIRE
HYDRANTS, ETC. PLEASE E-MAIL THE
CLONE CENTER IMMEDIATELY..
VIA: TRIMADIPOD@INT.COM

TRIMADIPOD

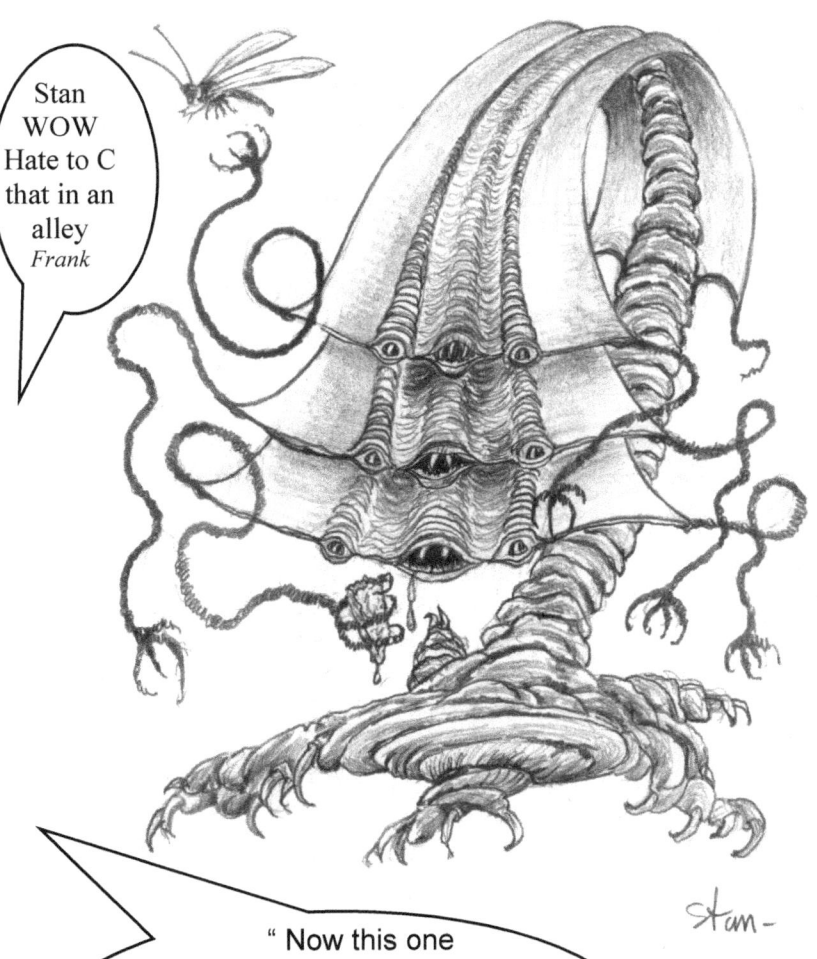

GUESS WHO WAS TAPPING ON MY WINDOW
PANE LAST NIGHT ? ..A LONG LOST FRIEND FROM AN
ALIEN FAMILY..ORIGINALLY HE WAS A "SEED EGG" GIFT.
GREW UP AND THEN WANDERED OFF,
BEFORE I GOT TO DRAW HIS PORTRAIT.
SADLY, WORD CAME BACK TO ME OF HIS
PASSING ..HE EVENTUALLY VISITED ME AS A FLOATING
ZOMBIE AND WANTED ME TO DRAW HIS PORTRAIT BUT
FOR A DIFFERENT REASON.
FLOATING ZOMBIES CANNOT SEE THEIR OWN MIRRORED
REFLECTION, SO I HAD TO DRAW HIM SO THAT HE
CAN VIEW HIS OWN IMAGE . BASICALLY ALIENS ARE
AFRAID OF
CAMERAS SO THATS WHAT ORIGINALLY STARTED
"MY ALIEN VISITORS".
ANOTHER INTERESTING FACT ALL ALIENS WHO VISIT ME,
GIFT ME WITH A "SEED EGG'"
EXCEPT THIS ALIEN ZOMBIE.
DON'T BE FRIGHTENED BY HIS APPEARANCE..
ACTUALLY HE IS SMILING. ALL HE ASKS OF
ME NOW, IS A PLACE
WHERE HE COULD "HANG OUT." I THOUGHT ABOUT
THIS AND THEN SUGGESTED WHY NOT RIGHT HERE IN
FLORIDA. WE HAVE MANY TREES THAT PROVIDE
SHADE ALL YEAR LONG ...WHY NOT "HANG OUT" IN A
TREE? YOU'LL GET LOTS OF FRESH AIR, SEE THE SUN
RISE AND SUN SET?
" GREAT IDEA ! " HE REMARKED
TO ME HE'S A GOOD SOUL WHO HAS
FOUND PEACE WITHIN.
WE CALL HIM

SOL

HI PEOPLE WELCOME CHERE

WE MET IN COMPUTER CHAT ROOM AN BECAME FRIENDS, SHE BOUGHT THE FIRST EDITION OF MY BOOK AND BECAME A FAN MEMBER. CHERE DID SHOW AN INTEREST IN BEING PART OF MY BOOK, OF COURSE THAT MEANT THE ALTERING OF HER DNA WITH A NEUCLEAR-GAMMA BIO ADJUSTMENT. SHE WAS EAGER TO START THE PROCESS, ALTHOUGH IT COULD BE DANGEROUS, I DID ADVISE AGAINST IT. BUT SHE IS A STUBBORN GAL , THEN THERE IS THE CARBO—FIBER REPLACEMENT REQUIREMENT TO HER BODY WHICH DOES PROVIDE THE DURABITITY TO ENDURE THE " BIO CENTRIFUGAL TRANSFORMATION PROCEEDURE " DURING THIS PROCESS. PHYSICAL CHANGES WILL OCCUR FORTUNATLY FOR CHERE THE END RESULT WAS AMAZING. HER TISSUE CHANGES BECAME PERFECTLY SYMMETRICAL. NO FACIAL, OR BODY DISTORTIONS. CHERE WAS THEN TRANSPORTED TO A RECEIVING PLATFORM FROM AN UNDISCLOSED LOCATION. THEN EARLY ONE MORNING I HEAR A TAPPING ON MY FRONT DOOR. THERE SHE WAS, ONE OF MY MENTAL IMAGES THAT APPEARED BEFORE ME.. AND THE FIRST THING SHE WANTED WAS FOR ME TO DRAW HER IMAGE. CHERE BEING A LONG TIME FRIEND, I WAS MORE THAN HAPPY TO OBLIGE. SHE THEN PLEADED WITH ME THAT SHE WANTED TO BE THE PAGE NEXT TO SOL, ONE OF HER FAVORITES...I HAVE LEARNED ONE THING FROM CHERE . NEVER ARGUE WITH A GAL ESPECIALLY A TRANSFORMED ONE.

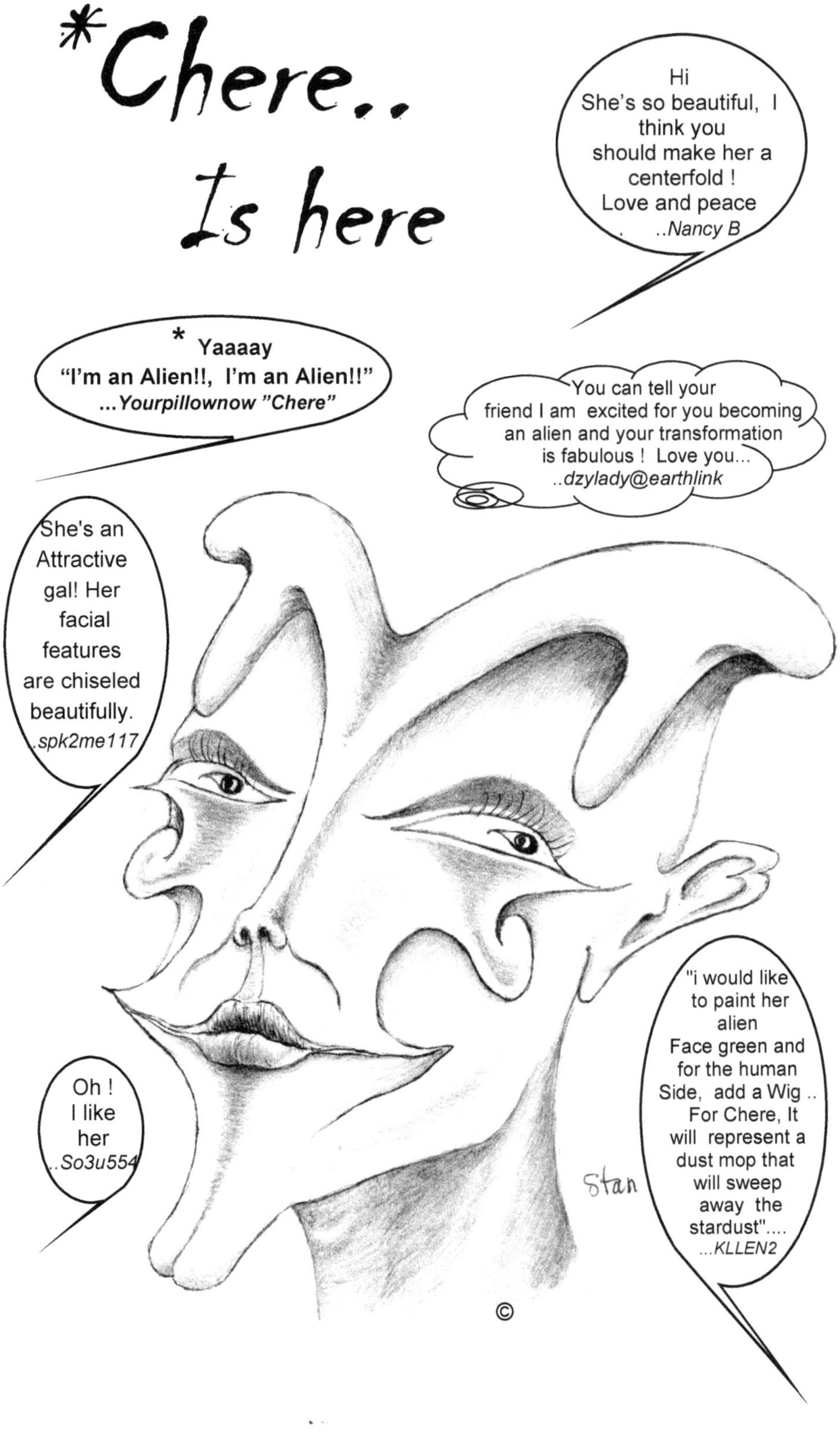
*Chere..
Is here
Hi She's so beautiful, I think you should make her a centerfold ! Love and peace ..Nancy B
* Yaaaay "I'm an Alien!!, I'm an Alien!!" ...Yourpillownow "Chere"
You can tell your friend I am excited for you becoming an alien and your transformation is fabulous ! Love you... ..dzylady@earthlink
She's an Attractive gal! Her facial features are chiseled beautifully. .spk2me117
Oh ! I like her ..So3u554
"i would like to paint her alien Face green and for the human Side, add a Wig .. For Chere, It will represent a dust mop that will sweep away the stardust".... ...KLLEN2
Stan
©

HERE SHE IS ..INFORMATION JUST ARRIVED ABOUT
LIBBY. YOU ARE LOOKING AT AN
UNFORTUNATE BIRTH DEFECT. SHE WAS SECRETLY
TRANSPORTED TO EARTH AT A YOUNG AGE WITH
HER MOTHER AND
FATHER, JUST AFTER THE ICE AGE ENDED ..THEY
WERE NOT HEARD FROM SINCE.
LIBBY'S REMAINS WERE DISCOVERED ABOUT
1790 IN NORTHERN FRANCE. ALIENS DO NOT TAKE
KINDLY TO   BIRTH DEFECTS. DURING HER BIRTH THE EGG
SPIKES DID NOT BREAK AWAY AT
EGG HATCHING TIME. WE TRIED TO CONTACT THE
B.C..R.C BIRTH CONTROL REGISTRY CENTER THEY WERE
NOT AVAILABLE FOR COMMENT
OH! BY THE WAY... ANOTHER ALIEN GAL WILL BE MAKING
HER PUBLIC APPEARANCE SOON . WHEN YOU SEE HER
JUST MAKE HER FEEL WELCOME

...STAN

Stan it seems to me that quite possibly
that LIBBY might have been an inspiration for famous
French statue in NYC. Its just a hunch. You may need to
investigate this further
...Lisa

LIBBY

GUESS WHAT HATCHED OUT LAST MONTH??
AN AQUA-MANDAPOID, BETTER KNOWN AS A POND WADER. IT WAS A SURPRISE GIFT FROM A PREVIOUS GUEST THAT ARRIVED HERE SOME TIME AGO. THE REAL PROBLEM IS TRANSPORTING, THIS CREATURE TO A LOCAL POND, I HAVE TO DO THIS UNDER COVER OF DARKNESS. ENVIRONMENTALLY IT'S A SURVIVAL CREATURE STANDING ABOUT 3 FEET HIGH. IN THE MEANTIME I HAVE TO KEEP ALL DOORS LOCKED UNTIL I'M READY TO MOVE IT OUT OF MY HOUSE. NORMALLY IT SEEKS OUT POND MOSQUITO LARVA AND WATER SKIMMING INSECTS. IT CAN DO THIS BECAUSE OF IT'S STRAW-LIKE APPENDAGES AS PART OF ITS MANDIBLE. WHEN IT'S IN MY HOUSE, IT WAS RAIDING MY FRIDGE FOR YOGURT, MILK AND COLA. FOR THOSE CONCERNED IT'S TOTALLY HARMLESS TO SMALL FISH, FROGS AND TURTLES, A NOTE TO ALL THOSE WHO WOULD LIKE TO CAPTURE IT, DON'T...
THIS IS NOT A PET. IT WON'T FOLLOW YOU AROUND THE HOUSE, COME WHEN IT'S CALLED, AND IT REFUSES TO BE HAND FED. AND IT WON'T HARM YOU. IT'LL JUST STARE AT YOU UNTIL YOU TRANSPORT IT TO A POND SITE.

Aqua- Mandapoid

HI PEOPLE, A NEW SOL IS IN TOWN WELCOME

Sol 2

HE HAS HEARD ABOUT THE FIRST SOLS SUCCESS AND
WANTS TO BE PART OF THE ACTION.
SO NOW SOL 2 IS INSISTING, THAT I FINISH THE
DRAWING AND PLACE HIM INTO REALITY
IMMEDIATELY. WHO WOULD IMAGINE THAT ONE OF MY
CREATIONS WOULD GET JEALOUS OF
THE ORIGINAL " SOL."
SOL 2 IS GETTING A BIT TOO MUCH FOR ME,
ESPECIALLY WHILE HE IS STILL BEING CREATED FROM MY
"MINDS EYE". I'M DRAWING HIM AS FAST AS I
CAN AND HE'S STILL COMPLAINING TO ME. " OK ! OK ! NOW ! "
WAIT ! I SAID, "I'M NOT FINISHED DRAWING YOU."
"YES ! YES ! YOU ARE ...STAN,

Oh my!!! A spooky little thing!!
Thank you for sharing doll.../
...........Kelley

oh, Sol 2, I see your
urgency for getting out here. a
handsome ghost like you is not to
be upstaged, even for a minute!
.....Yourpillownow

Wow, awesome
.Phantom of the opera playing
In my head now. "The Phantom
of the opera is there, inside my
mind" lol Cool drawing.
.......Jean

This ones my new favorite.
Maybe a little spooky for kids. it has
a forlorn atmosphere about it,
almost as though it were a ghost.
...   .OYamlandUO

Sol 2

ALIEN LOVERS, HERE SHE IS, ALIZA
SHE'S THE SISTER OF LIBBY.
WHEN YOU SEE ALIZA, PLEASE DONT MENTION
THOSE HEAD SPIKES, SHE'S VERY SENSITIVE
ABOUT THAT. IN FACT SHE'S
SEEING A PLASTIC SURGEON THIS VERY AFTERNOON,
IF HER GALACTIC HEALTH PLAN WOULD
COVER THE MEDICAL COSTS SHE WILL PAY A
VISIT TO HER FRIEND "DOGGYPADDLER" FOR
COFFEE, BROWNIES AND A CHAT ABOUT THE
BEST PLACES TO GO SHOPPING, AS WELL AS DOGGY'S
HAIR STYLE SUGGESTIONS. HER GREATEST
DESIRE WOULD BE TO GO SHOPPING WITH THE
GALS ON EARTH. SHE THINKS THEY ARE THE
COOLEST. SHE IS ALSO ANXIOUS TO BUY A
HAT AND EARRINGS OR EAR HANGING AS THEY
ALL THEM, WHICH WAS BORROWED FROM MY WIFE.
ALIZA WILL EVENTUALLY WILL BUY HER OWN PAIR.
...STAN

" You really need to
put this in a book, they would
be excellent reading as well as the artwork
It would be appealing and a nice book
...Pottergrl

" Aliza looks like
she enjoys flirting.
I think she is a bit
vain as well.
Luckily she is good
looking Except for, ...
(although I don't
mind them) "
...pucipaci "

Aliza

"I love her she is
so-cool
I bet she came from
one of those Alien
egg farms huh?"
La Rue VanGogh

" I think she's lovely
I'd love to take her Shopping Excessive
attention to ones minor physical flaws is mostly due to lack
of self esteem. I certainly wouldn't bring it up But, if I can get
her to open up, there's a chance that I could get her to like her
spikes they are part of what makes her unique and special "
....Doggypaddler

Hand-y eyes for the Aliens

THIS WAS DELIVERED TO MY CLONING
LABORATORY UNDER THE AUSPICES OF THE
U.A.C.C. DESIGNED FOR ALIENS WHO
HAVE LOST THEIR LEFT HAND AND EYES IN
BATTLE OR A WORKPLACE ACCIDENT, WILL BE
ELIGIBLE FOR THIS PROSTHESIS, PROVIDED
THEY HAVE A UNIVERSAL MEDICAL CARD. AS OF
NOW, ONLY THE LEFT HAND IS AVAILABLE.
WE ARE READY TO PROCESS ALL ORDERS.
DELIVERY WILL MADE AS SOON AS POSSIBLE.
EACH ORDER WILL HAVE A PERSONALIZED
CODE AND AN IMBEDDED THUMB PRINT
UNIQUE TO HE APPLICANTS ID.. INSTRUCTION
BOOKS, 4 BIO-OPTIC BRAIN CONNECTORS,
SKIN GLUE AND STAPLE KITS WILL BE
INCLUDED. SPECIAL FEATURES: THE EYES
ARE WATERPROOF SO IT'S SAFE TO
WASH YOUR HANDS OR SHOWER AS NECESSARY,
ALSO INCLUDED A BUILT -IN AUTO 180 / 0 ANGLE
EYE-SCAN. CONVENIENT WHEN TEXTING
WHILE OPERATING A
TRANSPORTER, ENTERING AN
UNKNOWN AREA.
THE HAND-Y EYES SEE FIRST.

HAND-Y EYES FOR THE ALIENS

AFTER I CREATED THIS CREATURE, WE THEN BOTH LOOKED AT EACH OTHER IN AMAZEMENT AND FOR A MOMENT I WAS SPEECHLESS AND ENTRANCED BY HER EYES. THE SIMILARITY OF JUST BEING BORN OR CREATED IS THAT BOTH ARE HUNGRY. SHE BEING A POLLEN EATER IMMEDIATELY STUFFS HER MOUTH WITH DIGESTABLE POLLEN FROM A NEARBY CLUSTER OF FLOWERS AND OF COURSE WAS UNABLE TO TALK.. I THEN TOLD HER, FOR HER SAFETY, TO STAY WITHIN THE GARDEN AREA UNTIL HER WINGS AND OTHER BODY PARTS BECOME FU LLY DEVELOPED. SHE THEN EXPRESSED HER THANKS BY COMING CLOSER TO ME, PLACING HER HEAD AGAINST MINE AND THEN GIVING ME A GENTLE BUZZING SOUND, NOTHING MORE. OUT OF RESPECT, I BUZZED HER BACK. NOW, WHAT TO NAME HER, BECAME MY NEXT CONCERN. MY DAUGHTER SUGGESTED SUGESTED THE NAME

" *Pauline* "

THIS SOUNDED PERFECT. WHEN I CALLED HER PAULINE, SHE THEN RESPONDED BY A SECOND HEAD BUZZING CONTACT. IT WAS OBVIOUS SHE LOVED THAT NAME . SHE WILL AFTER FULL DEVELOPMENT, FLY AWAY TO AN UNDISCLOSED LOCATION TO LAY *SEED-EGGS, TO INCREASE HER UNIQUE SPECIES. HOW SHE FIRST APPEARED TO ME ? IS A GOOD QUESTION. I WOULD SAY BY SOME IMAGINATIVE PROCESS, A CREATURE APPEARS ON MY DRAWING BOARD AND AS WITH ALL MY CREATIONS, THEY THEN TAKE ON A LIFE OF THEIR OWN.

*As you may already know my aliens present to selected humanoids A Seed-egg as a gift to hatch eggs at their convenience.

Pauline

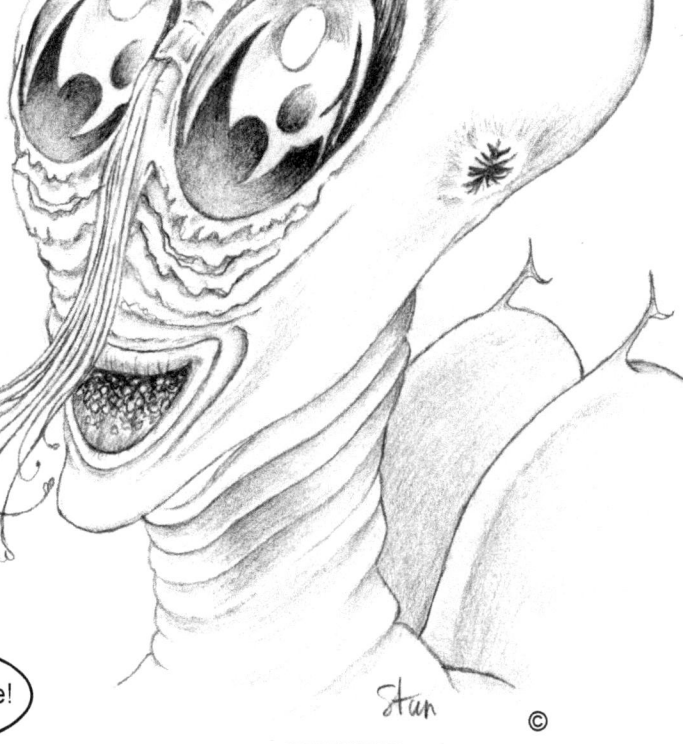

OK PEOPLE LETS ALL WELCOME A NEW CREATURE TO OUR FAMILY OF FRIENDS

Pleco

A GENTLE POOL FRIENDLY PLAYMATE WHO LOVES TO MINGLE WITH POOL SWIMMERS AS WELL AS " POOL PLAYERS " AND KOI - CARP FISH. THIS BREED OF PLECO, WILL HARMLESSLY CRAWL OVER YOU, TO GET TO YOUR OTHER SIDE. BASICALLY THE PLECO IS A BOTTOM AND MID-WAY FEEDER THAT LEAVES "NOTHING BEHIND." A NOSTRIL WATER BREATHER WITH ITS TOTAL BODY GILL SURFACE, THAT RELEASES OUT CLEAN WATER. ITS MAIN ENVIRONTMENTAL REQUIREMENT IS THAT THE POOL WATER DOES NOT CONTAIN ANTI-ALGAE OR ANY OTHER CHEMICALS. ..IT WILL THEN GRADUALLY TRANSFORM YOUR POOL INTO A SWIMMABLE AQUARIUM, WHERE YOU CAN ENJOY AND SAFELY SWIM WITH PLECO AND HIS KOI COD FISH PALS COMPANIONS, WHO YOU CAN FEED WHILE SWIMMING. THE PLECO WILL SIMPLY PICK UP AND CONSUME THE LEFTOVER FOOD. HIS FISH KOI FRIENDS WILL SIMPLY PECK ON HIM TO KEEP HIM CLEAN. THIS PLECO WAS ORIGINALLY GIFTED TO ME AS A NEW SPECIES SEED-EGG FROM DUPUS, ANOTHER ALIEN POOL FRIEND. PLECO IS A TOUGH ALL WEATHER SURVIVOR AND HAS THE ABILITY TO HYBERNATE AS LONG AS THE POOL WATER, DOES NOT FREEZE TO THE BOTTOM.

Your work is very distinct
With your own "stanview" Thanks
P.S. May I use the image in my blog replate
with your description & the usual copy-
right ?
..... *kungpaoyak*

nice stan, Interesting
creature.....I'm Sure you enjoy
The hobby of drawing
them. Thanks for sending.
.....*Dreadlox33*

Hey ! that's a great idea.
We are having a pool
constructed in our back yard.
A Pleco would be a delightful
welcomed guest..who will
also keep the pool clean.
.............*Brenda*

you are,the father of Pleco. I love him
he's awesome, love his eyes love everything
about him. I get overwhelmed about how
talented you are. Stan, you are amazing
.... *Yourpillownow*

The eyes are
not quite alluring enough
....*Skeeknlin*

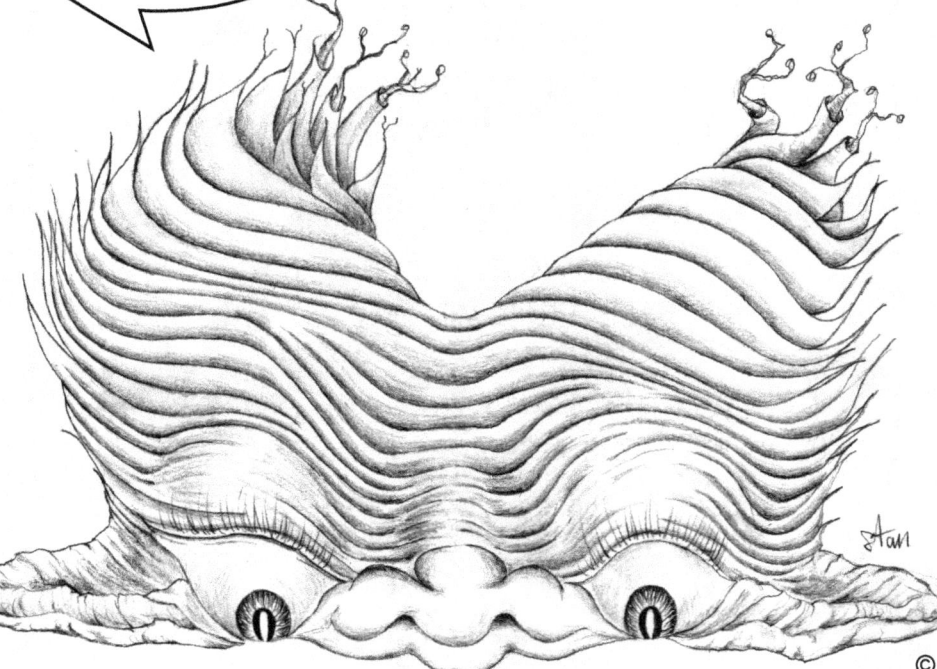

WELL OUR GAL WENT AND DID IT. RATHER
THAN WAIT FOR THE GROUP TO HELP HER
SHOP FOR THE LATEST FASHIONS SHE
GOES OUT HERSELF. SHE WALKS INTO A
COSTUME
STORE IN LOWER MANHATTAN, NYC., AND
PURCHASED A HAT, AND DIDN'T REALIZE
IT'S A FUN CLOWN HAT. ALIZA IS ONE OF THE
ALIEN GALS THAT HAS SUFFERED
WITH HEAD SPIKES THAT DIDN'T FALL OFF
AFTER HATCHING. SHE'S HAPPY SHE FINALLY
HAD THOSE SPIKES REMOVED A WHILE
BACK AND THAT HAT ENDED UP FITTING LIKE A
GLOVE, AND
SHE LOVES IT...WELL, LET ME TELL YOU THIS, ...
WHEN THE GALS SAW THAT, THEY STARED AT
HER IN AMAZEMENT. THE BEST REACTION SHE
GOT WAS A "VERY NICE." THEY
KNOW THE UNWRITTEN RULE; NEVER
CRITIZE WHAT OTHER GALS OR OR ALIEN
LADIES WEAR. THE GIRLS WERE NICE TO HER,
MADE HER FEEL AT HOME, IN FACT MY ON-LINE
FRIEND "DOGGYPADDLER, "
INVITED HER TO PLAY A GAME OF CANASTA
WITH A GROUP OF LADIES.
OH YES ! AND THIS GAL ALIZA, WILL
" DISH THE DIRT WITH THE GIRLS "

WELL HERE IS THE FULL STORY ON THIS GUY.
IM THE MIDDLE OF DRAWING THIS FELLOW HE BECAME
IMPATIENT AND LEFT MY DRAWING BOARD. HE HAS HEARD ABOUT
AN ALIEN SOCIAL EVENT WITHIN WALKING WHILE CROSSING THE
STREET HE HAD AN ALTERCATION WITH A SPEEDING CAR...
HE DAMAGED HIS HEAD AN OTHER BODY PARTS AN
NATURALLY HE THEN CRAWLED TO NEAREST AUTO BODY
SHOP FOR REPAIR.. ALL THEY DID WAS APPLY A
SHEEET METAL BAND AID .. THAT DIDN'T HELP SO HE
WAS TRANSPORTED TO A SECRET ALIEN HOSPITAL.
HE LOVES HIS FREEDOM AND HE'S NOT COMING BACK TO
THE DRAWING BOARD. SO I NEVER GOT THE CHANCE TO
NAME HIM OR EVEN SIGN THE DRAWING.

Hello patient # 333004453,
welcome to our health facility. After
our lab checked you over we have a
list of your damaged body parts, we
cannot heal them but fortunately for
you, we have
replaceable alien body parts and
under the "Universal / Replaceable parts
Heath Care System" all is taken
care of. My name is Markus and I
will be your intern.
Being an alien myself, I understand the
replacement process. I have made a
list of all your replaceable parts. Your
forehead of course will be bone
welded back into shape
after we
remove the metal band aid.
After a few weeks you will be
almost as good as new.

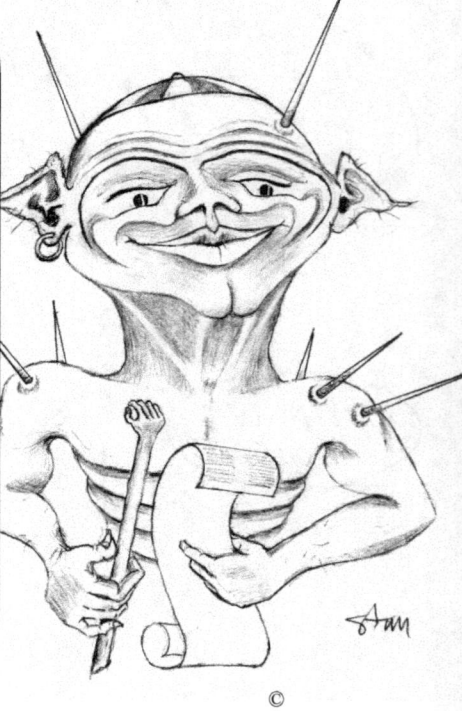

©

With so many great suggestions,
perhaps you can check your
own favorite names ✓

- ☐ Al
- ☐ Bogustoff
- ☐ Bumper
- ☐ Casper
- ☐ Gustpoh
- ☐ Jeffery
- ☐ Jimmy
- ☐ Mendid
- ☐ Old Guy
- ☐ Pigman
- ☐ Spork
- ☐ Yoda

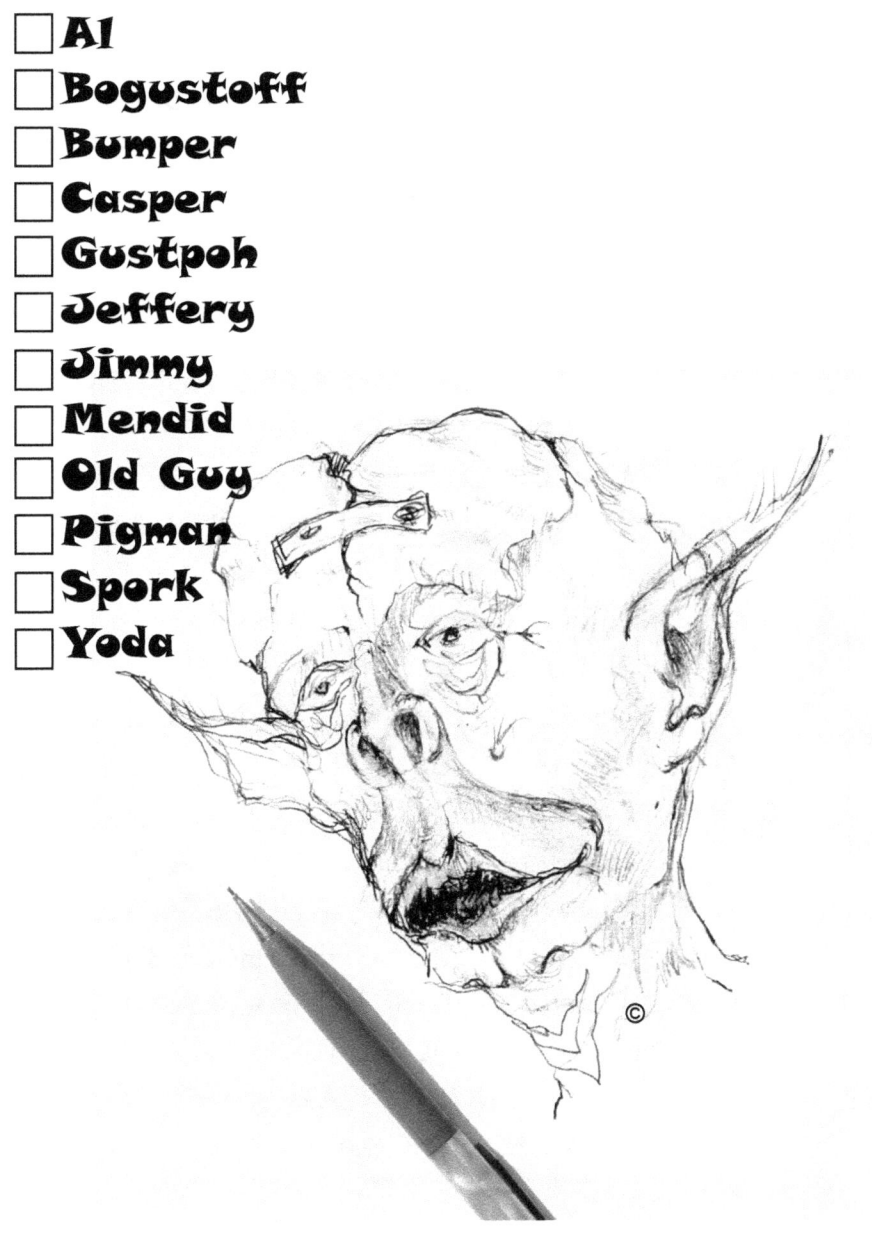

OK PEOPLE
INTRODUCING THE SMART CAT, THE IDEAL
COMPANION FOR ANY ALIEN. EASY TO FEED,
ALTHOUGH IT WILL ACCEPT CANNED FOOD,
IT DOES HOWEVER
PREFER "FRESH" ROAD KILL .
IF THIS SMART PET WANTS A NICE SALAD ,
ALL SHE HAS TO DO IS EAT THE SALAD EATER ..
IT MAKES PERFECT SENSE. INSTEAD OF
SPENDING ALL DAY GRAZING ON GRASS, IT
COULD HAVE THE EQUIVALENT OF THAT IN
20 MINUTES OF EATING. SHE THINKS
VEGETARIANS ARE SILLY, THERE'S NOTHING
BETTER THAN "FRESH" ROAD KILL.
HER DOMESTICATED FELINE PALS HAVE NOT
SEEN THE ERROR OF THEIR WAYS...CANNED
FOOD FOR CATS AND MILK ? ENOUGH TO
MAKE ONE GAG...ANYWAY ENOUGH OF THIS,,,,
FOR FUN, SHE TEASES DOGS ...
ALL SHE HAS TO DO IS MAKE HER HAIR STAND
ON END. THAT WILL MAKE THE BIGGEST
DOG RUN FOR COVER, ANOTHER TRICK UP HER
FURRY SLEVE; SHE'LL PLAY DEAD AND
WHEN A DOG COMES OVER AND STARTS
SNIFFING,SHE WILL OPEN THOSE BIG
EYES OF HERS AND GROWL THEN YOU'LL
SEE THE DOG ACTUALLY FAINT ..OH ! THIS
IS JUST GREAT
SPORT FOR THE SMART PET .

Smart Pet

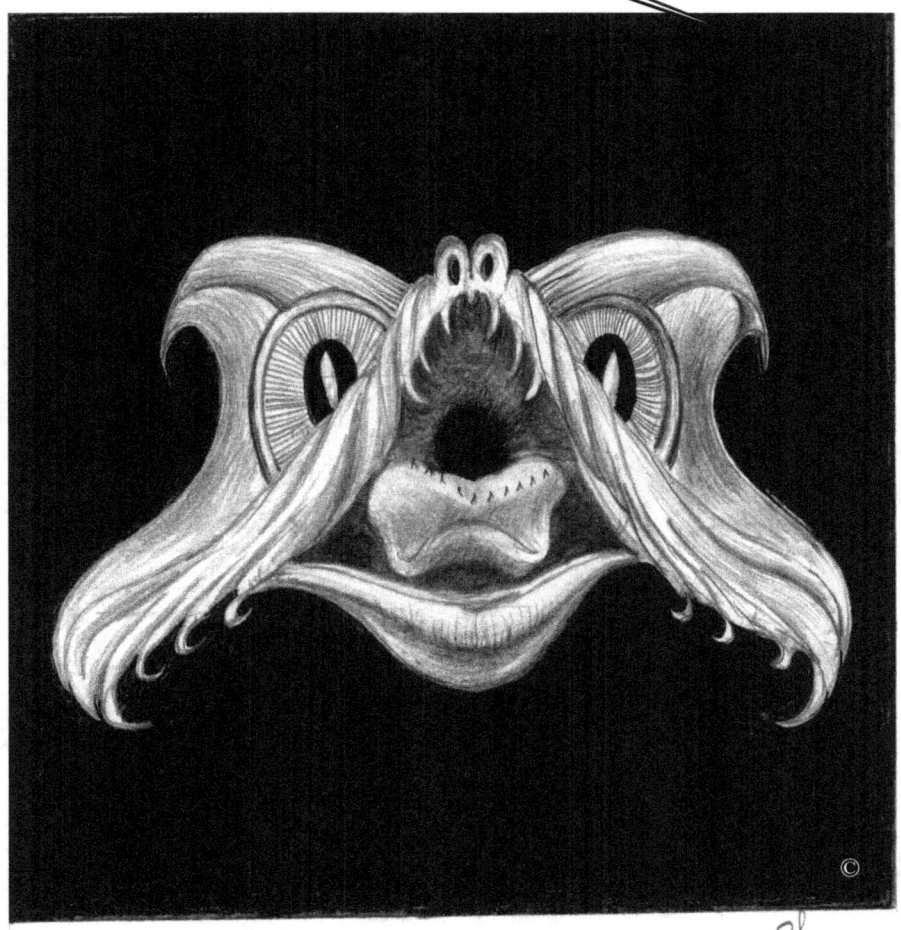

SOME YEARS AGO, I RECEIVED BY
SPECIAL ESCORT
A VERY YOUNG CHILD, 4 YEARS OF AGE
FROM A "SEED-EGG." HOWEVER DURING HIS STAY
AT THE LABORATORY HOSPITAL FOR
DEVELOPMENT, AN UNFORTUNATE DEFORMITY
TOOK PLACE. HE WILL NOW RESIDE IN MY HOUSE FOR
REST AND REHABILITATION. NOW AFTER ALMOST 2
YEARS HE'S DOING NICELY, WITHIN TWO WEEKS
HIS MOM WILL TAKE HIM BACK HOME.

A LOVING, FRIENDLY AND INTELLIGENT BOY,
6 YEARS OF AGE. HE IS SHOWING INTEREST
MATHEMATICS. AND IS HELPFUL AROUND THE HOUSE.
BILLY WAS LOOKING INTENTLY AT MY DRAWINGS
ON THE WALL, FROM MY PAST VISITORS, HE THEN
ASKED ME TO DRAW HIS PORTRAIT.

"I think this kid will have a split personality.
Perhaps keeping him on a potassium based drug will
facilitate information transfer speed between both brain halves
and allow him to function—that he will be clearly one side
dominant and the other being prisoner.—
it works for some."
......Mike F.

Billy Boy

WELL THIS LITTLE FELLA FAKES KITE ACTION,
WITHOUT WINGS OR STRING ATTACHMENTS.
IT WILL TAKE TO THE SKY WITH THE WIND OR
THERMAL HEAT COLUMN AND HOVER LIKE
A KITE. IT CAN BOB, WEAVE, DIP, TWIRL,
SHIMMY AND SHAKE, WITH THE BEST OF THEM,
IT'S AN AEROTICK.
IT SOARS HIGH TOWARD THE SUN AND THEN
DROPS LIKE AN EAGLE TO "DROPCATCH"
HAWKS IN FLIGHT WITH ITS MOUTH OPEN
WITHOUT A SOUND, SO CLAWS ARE
UNNECESSARY. TRUTHFULLY I HAVE NO IDEA
WHERE THIS CAME FROM. PROBABLY A
FORGOTTEN TOY
FROM A PAST ALIEN VISITOR.
THE LOCAL CHICKEN FARMERS CALL IT
" THE BLACK KITE. "
THEY ARE NOT TOO CONCERNED BECAUSE THE
AEROTICK LIKES HAWKS, SO THEIR CHICKENS
ARE SAFE. WHEN THE WIND DIMINISHES,
THE AEROTICK
WILL THEN GLIDE TO THE TALLEST TREE AND
BECOME THE
" KITE CAUGHT IN THE TREE, "
UNTIL NEXT MORNING SUNRISE.

Aerotick

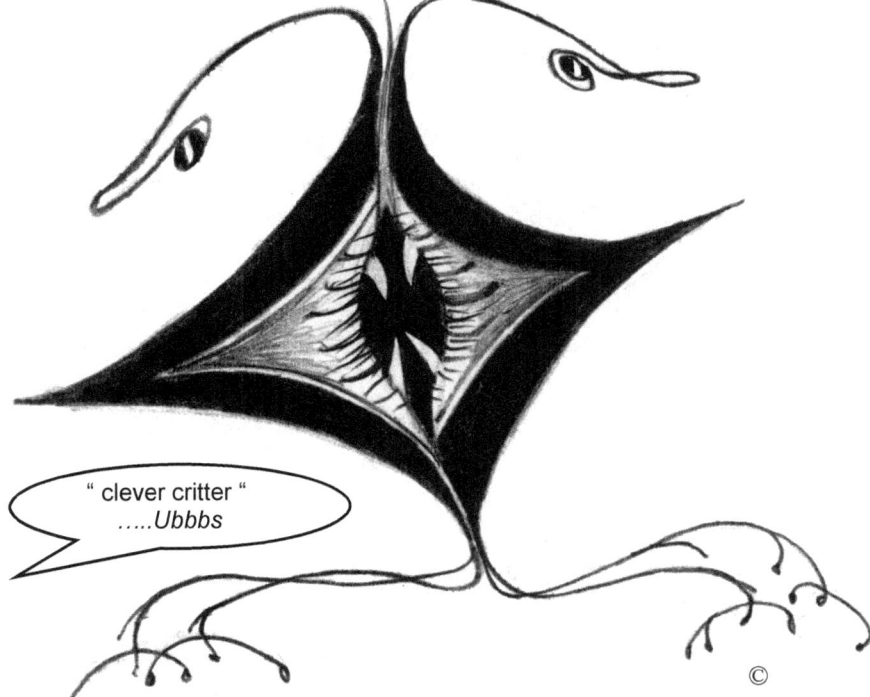

OK PEOPLE, HERE WE HAVE A TREE-CREATURE, THAT WAS RECENTLY DISCOVERED ON AN ALIEN LANDSCAPE. IT HAS NO OFFICAL NAME, SO FOR NOW WERE CALLING IT ●●●.

IT WAS A GIFT DELIVERY FROM A PAST ALIEN VISITOR, NOT AS A "SEED EGG" BUT AS A VOLUNTARY TREE CUTTING FROM THE MOTHER PLANT. MY INSTRUCTIONS WERE TO PLACE IT IN A WARM LOCATION AND WITHIN A FEW WEEKS IT GREW LEGS AND BECAME MOBILE. DURING THAT STAGE IT WILL FEED ITSELF THROUGH AN OPENING IN ITS OUTER SURFACE, WHICH THEN CLOSES UP, ONCE WE CAN FIND A FERTILE EARTH LOCATION. ITS LEGS WILL THEN DEVELOPED ROOTS INTO THE EARTH. TRANS-FORMING ITSELF INTO A TREE-CREATURE. IT WILL DEVELOP CHAMELEON- LIKE ABILITIES SO IT CAN COLOR-BLEND WITH THE SURROUNDING PLANTS.

●●●

HAS 3 EYES AROUND ITS CYLINDRICAL TREE TRUNK, TO HELP IT SEE AND CAPTURE FLYING INSECTS. IT WILL THEN BURY ITS FOOD JUST BELOW THE EARTH SURFACE. THIS HELPS KEEP THE SOIL IN NUTRITIONAL CONDITION. TO REPRODUCE, IT WILL REMOVE A PIECE OF ITSELF TO GROW INTO ANOTHER

●●●,

AND IT WILL BECOME THE MOTHER, WHO WILL CARE FOR THIS NEW TREE-CREATURE. THE RESEARCH TEAM HAVE NOW DECIDED GIVE IT A LATIN NAME. THEY THOUGHT THE ORIGINAL NAME WAS A BIT DIFFICULT TO PRONOUNCE, SO THEY AGREED ON

"ARBOREUS MOBILIS"

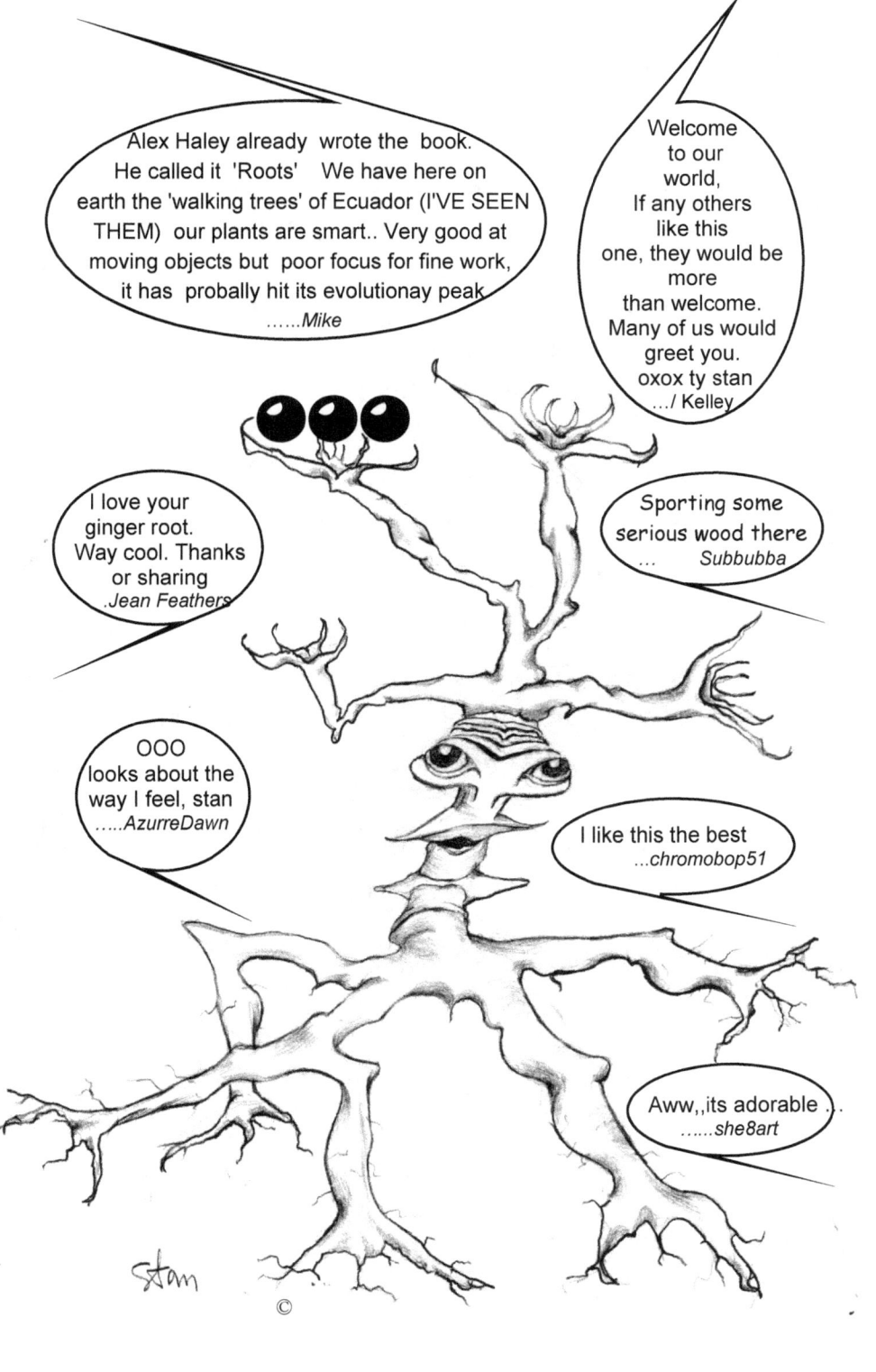

WELL WHAT CAN I SAY ABOUT THIS
A SWEETHEART OF A LADY, SHE INTRODUCED
HERSELF AS BELLA, THE MOTHER OF
MORRIS WHO WAS BLESSED WHEN
MORRIS AND MANDY
HAD THEIR FIRST BORN
MATTHEW
SHE TALKED ABOUT MORRIS' YOUNGER DAYS
WHEN HE WAS A LAZY GOOD FOR NOTHING DAY
DREAMER, AND WANDERER, HOW HE POUTED
WITH THAT ONE.
ANYWAY SHE'S HAPPY WITH MATTHEW.
A BEAUTIFUL GRANDCHILD AND
THANKED ME FOR CARING FOR HIM DURING AND
AFTER HATCHING . BEFORE COMING HERE SHE
GOT ALL DRESSED UP AND
PURCHASED A SUNHAT AND DRESS. I WAS
ABOUT TO TELL HER ABOUT THAT
INAPPROPRIATE
TAG ON HER DRESS, WHEN IN HER JOY ,
SHE SAID THE
DRESS TAG WAS AN EXCELLENT DESIGN
TOUCH.
I JUST KEPT MY MOUTH SHUT. SHE WAS
ALSO EXCITED ABOUT VISITING NYC AND
THE STATUE OF LIBERTY.
\SHE SAID, IT REMINDED HER OF
HER NIECE, LIBBY..

Grandma Bella

Carl

ACCIDENTS DO HAPPEN. A CREATURE EMERGED FROM A
SEED-EGG GIFT WITH BULGING EYES. IT WAS SUPPOSED TO
HATCH INTO A NORMAL ALIEN I THEN REALIZED I MIGHT
HAVE STORED IT TOO CLOSE TO
MY MICROWAVE OVEN. FORTUNATELY FOR ME PARENTS
CONSIDER THEIR OFFSPRING BEAUTIFUL BUT WHO AM I TO
SAY OTHERWISE. AS FOR THAT BROKEN ANTENNA, THAT WILL
RE-GROW. ANYWAY SINCE I'M THE OFFICIAL HATCHER I'M GIVIN
THE PRIVILEGE OF NAMING HIM CARL, HAPPY AND SMILING AND
THAT'S ALL THAT MATTERS TO ME. HIS EGG LAYING PARENTS
SHOULD ARRIVE HERE IN A FEW
DAYS I'LL THEN RECEIVE ANOTHER EGG-SEED REWARD. A GIFT
FOR MY ALIEN PORTRAIT DRAWING SERVICE, WHICH I AM
HONORED THAT I HAVE ACHIEVED INTER-PLANETARY ACCLAIM
AND SINCE CARL IS ACTUALLY AFRAID OF OUR TRANSPORTATION.
WE HAVE TO TAKE LONG HIKES VISITING FARMS FOR FOOD.
CARL LIKES TO EATS; APPLES, PEARS, AND HIS AND MY
FAVORITE IS TOMATOES. MOST OTHER FRUITS HAVE
A HARD SKIN, BUT AS A SPECIAL TREAT I WILL OPEN A CAN OF
TOMATO SAUCE THAT WE BOTH CAN SHARE. CARL IS HAPPY,
BEING OUR HOUSE PET GUEST. AS SOON AS THE PUP SAW
IM, SHE JUMPED INTO HIS LAP, IMMEDIATE FRIENDSHIP.
I APPRECIATE IT WHEN CARL TAKES OUR PUP OUT FOR A WALK,
BARKING AND CHATTING TOGETHER , AN AMUSING
SIGHT TO SEE. THE NEIGHBORS SEE THIS AND THEY GET
UPSET. PET GUESTS NEED OTHER PETS TO CARE FOR. SO
WHEN CARL GETS BACK HOME HIS PARENTS WILL GIFT
HIM A PET FOR HIS VERY OWN. WELL THAT TIME HAS FINALLY
ARRIVED TO TAKE CARL HOME. AND
SADLY ENOUGH BEFORE LEAVING HE LOOKED BACK AT ME
WITH BLUE TEARS IN HIS EYES AND WAVED GOODBYE, CARL
THEN HUGGED THE PUP AND HE LEFT. OUR PUP WAS SADLY
ROAMING THE HOUSE LOOKING FOR HIM BUT AFTER A
FEW DAYS SHE WAS FINALLY BACK TO HER OLD SELF.

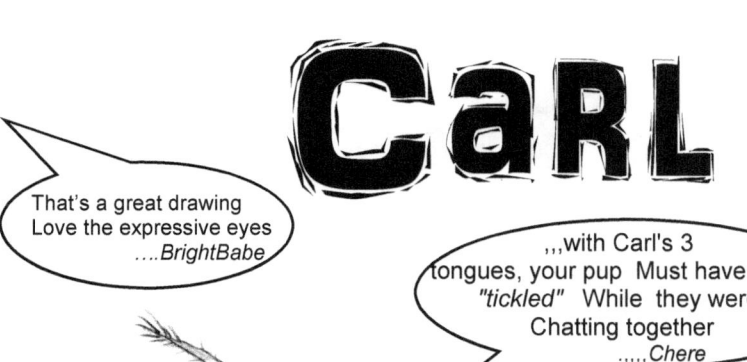

HI PEOPLE
GUESS WHO DROPPED OVER LAST NIGHT ?
IT WAS ALEX. HE WAS LOOKING FOR HIS
GIRL FRIEND BELLA, TO HELP HIM AND IN TURN,
HE PROMISED TO BE GOOD TO HER.
RECENTLY HE JUST GOT FIRED FROM HIS FIRST
EVENING OF EMPLOYMENT AS HOUSE BUTLER.
HE MANAGED TO PUT THE
ENTIRE DINNER PARTY INTO SHOCK, WHEN HE
ANNOUNCED "DINNER IS SERVED
" TOTALLY NAKED.
NEEDLESS TO SAY, ALL THE LADIES
FAINTED AND THE GUYS JUST TOSSED HIM
OUT THE DOOR. HE THEN SHOWS UP AT THE
UNEMPLOYMENT OFFICE THE SAME WAY. THE
GUARDS THREW A TARP OVER HIM AND
DELIVERED HIM TO MY HOUSE. FROM THERE I
TOLD HIM TO STAY ON THE PORCH UNDER
WRAPS UNTIL BELLA COMES TO GET HIM.
SHE THEN THANKED ME AND AS A
GIFT, SHE PRESENTED TO ME A "SEED-EGG" FOR
FUTURE HATCHING. I DECIDED TO DRAW HIS
IMAGE FROM THE WAIST UP.
YOU CAN UNDERSTAND WHY .

Alex

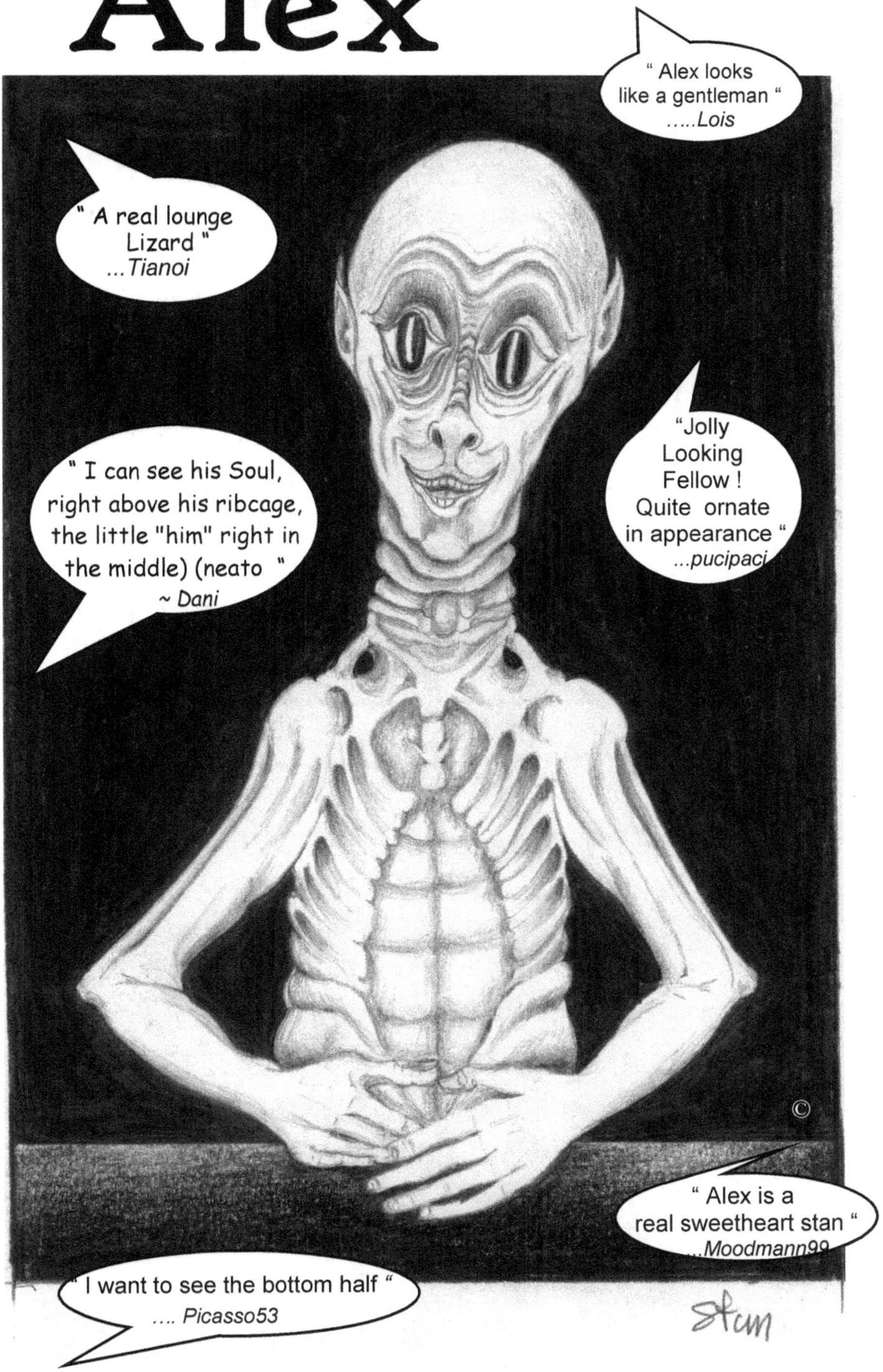
" Alex looks like a gentleman " .....Lois
" A real lounge Lizard " ...Tianoi
"Jolly Looking Fellow ! Quite ornate in appearance " ...pucipaci
" I can see his Soul, right above his ribcage, the little "him" right in the middle) (neato " ~ Dani
©
" Alex is a real sweetheart stan " ...Moodmann99
" I want to see the bottom half " Picasso53
Stan

oDEx

WELCOME ODEX
AN HONORED PET OF THE MORRIS FAMILY. A
HOUSE PROTECTER AGAINST ALL INTRUDERS. AT
NIGHT IT HOVER'S QUIETLY AND NEVER LEAVES
RESIDUE. IT SLEEPS ON THE UNDERSIDE OF THE
OWNERS BED. IF ODEX HEARS A DISTURBANCE
OUTSIDE, NO NEED FOR CONCERN, IT WILL
IMMEDIATELY CLIMB TO THE FOOT OF THE BED
AND STAND GUARD. IN THE WILD, IT
RESTS ON THE SIDE OF CLIFF ROCKS.
A DEPENDABLE PET TO HAVE AROUND THE
HOUSE. SO ORDER YOUR HOUSE PET NOW..
WHILE THEY ARE STILL AVAILABLE.

IT IS GENETICALLY BLESSED WITH EYES IN
CIRCUMFERENCE, SO IT DOESN'T HAVE TO TURN
AROUND AND LEAVE ITSELF UNAWARE OF
PREDATORS APPROACHING. IN ADDITION TO
PROTECT ITSELF, ALL IT HAS TO DO IS CLOSE
ALL EYES AND MOUTHS AND DISGUISE ITSELF TO
LOOK LIKE A POISONOUS MUSHROOM CAP AND
BE SAFE FROM IT'S ENEMIES. THE MALES
HOWEVER, ARE FREE ROAMERS SO IT'S THE
FEMALES THAT MAKE THE BEST
HOUSE PROTECTORS.

...STAN.

ONE THING A ODEX PET OWNER MUST
UNDERSTAND IS THAT AN ODEX IS HAPPY IF
IT HAS A PET OF ITS OWN. KEEP IN MIND
THAT A HAPPY PET WORKS WITH ENTHUSIASM
IN PROTECTING YOU, EVEN WHEN
YOU'RE SLEEPING. IT WILL DISPOSE OF ALL
INTRUDERS WITHOUT A TRACE.
ODEX'S PET HAS NO NAME FOR A GOOD
REASON, BECAUSE THIS PET
ONLY RESPONDS TO HER
WITH A SERIES OF CODED CLICKS.
SO FOR A HAPPY PET, AND FOR ALL ODEX
OWNERS, ORDER YOUR "PET FOR A PET"
AS SOON AS POSSIBLE.
YOU'LL NEVER HAVE TO FEED IT.
ODEX WILL TAKE CARE OF THAT.
NEVER OFFER FOOD TO THE PET'S PET. SHE CAN
GET VERY JEALOUS, IT WAS MEANT FOR HER
ALONE, TO CARE FOR. SO KEEP CHILDREN
AWAY FROM ODEX'S PET. BECAUSE CHILDREN
MIGHT BE TEMPTED TO OFFER IT FOOD.
IN THE ILLUSTRATION AS SHOWN, YOU
CAN SEE HOW ODEX IS FEEDING IT,
NOTICE THE LOVE AND PATIENCE,
SHE HAS FOR HER PET.

"Gruesome!
TiaNoi "

" I like the feeding
I think its cool "
SequiturAL

"A Pet for ODEX"

Ms. Universe
Jillian

SHE WAS TRANSPORTED TO ME LAST NIGHT AS
ANOTHER EGG HEAVY GAL. AS FAR AS TH
HATCHING CARE IS CONCERNED,
EACH EGG IS TREATED WITH THE SAME LOVE AND
CARE, NO MATTER WHO LAYS THE SEED-EGG. THIS
IS CALLED " UNIVERSAL CARE. "
I WAS GIVEN THE SAME HONOR TO CARE FOR ALL
SEED-EGGS LEFT WITH ME THIS IS WHY
JILLIAN AND STELLA ARE
ALLOWING ME TO BE THE EGG GUARDIAN. AS
YOU ALL REMEMBER, I WAS WITH SETH DURING
HIS INCUBATION AND HATCHING. NOW JILLIAN
WANTS TO BE A FASHION MODEL, AS SHE
HAS DONE SOME MODELING ON HER SIDE O
THE UNIVERSE. SINCE ALIENS ARE
AFRAID OF CAMERAS, THEY WILL ALLOW ONLY
HUMAN ARTISTS TO DRAW THEM.JILLIAN IS NOW
DOING A BIT OF   NUDE POSING FOR ME
FOR HER PORTFOLIO. HOWEVER, MY
WIFE PUT A STOP TO THAT. NOW I'LL
HAVE TO SEEK OUT
ANOTHER ARTIST TO FINISH THE WORK.

Jillian

BECAUSE OF STOCKHOLDER DEMAND AND CONTINUED PRODUCTION TO INCREASE SALES AND BECAUSE WE HAVEN'T RECEIVED OUR USUAL SHIPMENT FROM ANOTHER CLONING CORPORATION, OUR STAFF TOOK MATTERS IN THEIR OWN HANDS AND NOT WAIT FOR DELIVERY. THEY GATHERED UP BIO TISSUE DNA, SOME LEFT OVER STEM CELLS AND FILTERED FORMULA PROTEIN MIX, AND CREATED THIS DUO MANDABLOID CREATURE. WE CONSIDER IT VERY SALEABLE IT'S THE ONLY "NON SEED-EGG" CREATION BEING MARKETED. THERE ARE SOME BUGS TO WORK OUT, THE MAIN PROBLEM IS THAT OCCASSIONALLY, IT BITES ITS OWN TONGUE. UNFORTUNATELY IT DOESN'T GROW BACK. THAT IS SORT OF EMBARRASSING. ANOTHER FAULT, IT CANNOT HEAR COMMANDS. APPARENTLY AN EYE WAS CLONED IN THE EAR BY MISTAKE AND THIS WILL TAKE A FEW MONTHS TO CORRECT. TRUTHFULLY WE HAVE NO CURRENT USE FOR THIS PRODUCTION PIECE. WE MAY JUST ABANDON IT. STILL IT'S NOWHERE AS BAD AS THE "REJECT" DISASTER. AT LEAST WE WOULDN'T GET FIRED, IT COULD HOWEVER BE DONATED AS A SCHOOL CROSSING GUARD, OF COURSE WE WOULD HAVE TO REMOVE THE COMPANY LABEL . A REAL DUO-MANDA-"BLUNDER"

Duo-Mandabloid

WELL, WHAT CAN I SAY
AS YOU ALL MUST KNOW ABOUT
\QUASIMODO'S MOTHER,
WHO DROPPED OFF A SECRET "SEED-EGG" TO
A PREVIOUS EGG RECEIVER BEFORE ME.
ANDRIOUS DID HATCH OUT, AND AS
THE STORY GOES, WOULD HAVE
NEVER ACHIEVED ANYTHING IF, NOT
FOR THE THOUGHTFULNESS OF HIS OLDER
BROTHER QUASIMODO, THE NOTRE DAME
BELL RINGER. WHO SO GENEROUSLY OFFERED
YOUNG ANDRIOUS A START IN THE
CASTLE KITCHEN, AND FOR THAT, ANDRIOUS
WAS FOREVER INDEBTED TO HIS OLDER
BROTHER. NOW ANDRIOUS BEING
HANDICAPPED, ALTHOUGH NOT AS SEVERE AS
HIS OLDER BROTHER, ONLY HAS A WEAK EYE,
NECK AND LEG DEVELOPMENT PROBLEMS
OTHERWISE,
HE'S IN PERFECT CONDITION.

. TO BRING YOU UP TO DATE, THIS IS
WHERE ANDRIOUS EXCELLED,
WITH HIS FAMOUS DESSERT CREATION,
WELL KNOWN THROUGHOUT THE KINGDOM.
A PERFECT FINISH AFTER
EATING VENISON, EVER SINCE THEN,
HIS REWARD WAS, THAT HE NEVER AGAIN
HAD TO HAUL OUT THE GARBAGE.

A RECENTLY DISCOVERED ANDRIOUS
DELICIOUS DESSERT RECIPE, WAS FINALLY
MADE PUBLIC: CONSISTING OF; EGGS,
PIG FAT, HONEYCOMB AND GINGER.

Andrious

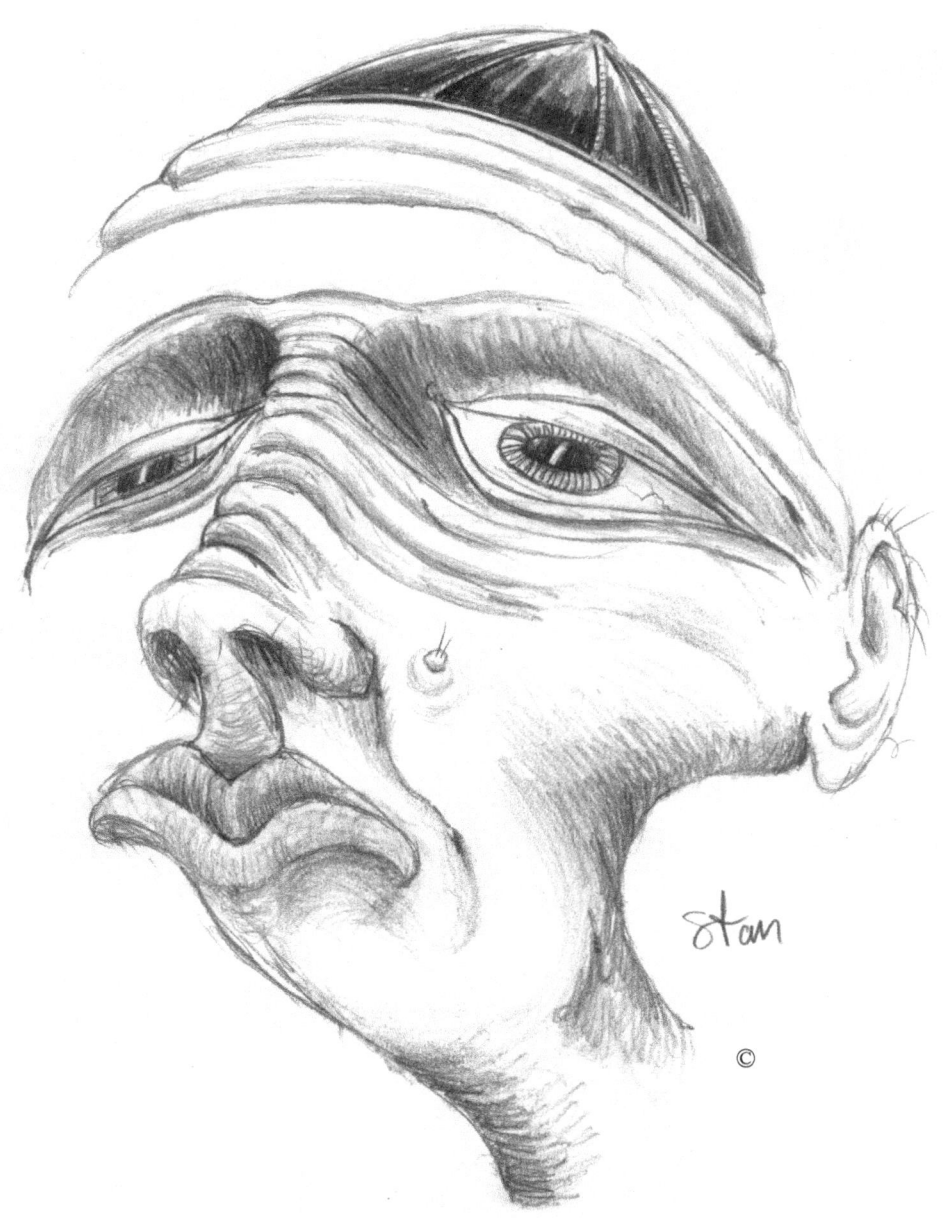

HI PEOPLE.
..MEET KEBOB, AN ORFACTOID.
THIS LI'L FELLER WAS THE FIRST IN THE
HATCHING FROM TWO "SEED-EGGS" I'VE
RECEIVED FROM MORRIS COUSIN, VINCENT...
FORTUNATELY BEFORE BONDING TO ME,
I HAD TO TRANSPORT KEBOB ......TO ANY HOME
OR THEATRE WITH A LARGE VIEWING
SCREEN ..I HAVE A SPECIAL WAY OF HOLDING
HIM, IT'S THE 5TH GROOVE DOWN FROM THE
EYE BROW RIDGE AND IT THEN BECOMES
DOCILE. ...KEBOB WOULD LOVE TO LIVE
WHERE HE CAN SPEND HIS
DAYS BONDING TO FAMOUS SCREEN ACTORS.
BETWEEN EACH MOVIE KEBOB,
WILL EAT FLOOR DROPPED POPCORN..SO
KEEP LARGE SUPPLY HANDY AND OH YES!
BEFORE I FORGET...KEBOB'S FAVORITE SEAT
IS THE 5TH ROW CENTER.

" Looks like his eye
sockets will be easy for him to see the
big screen and all its action. ..All he needs
his own box of pop corn poor Orfactoid
not eating off the floor ".
...La RueVan Gogh,,

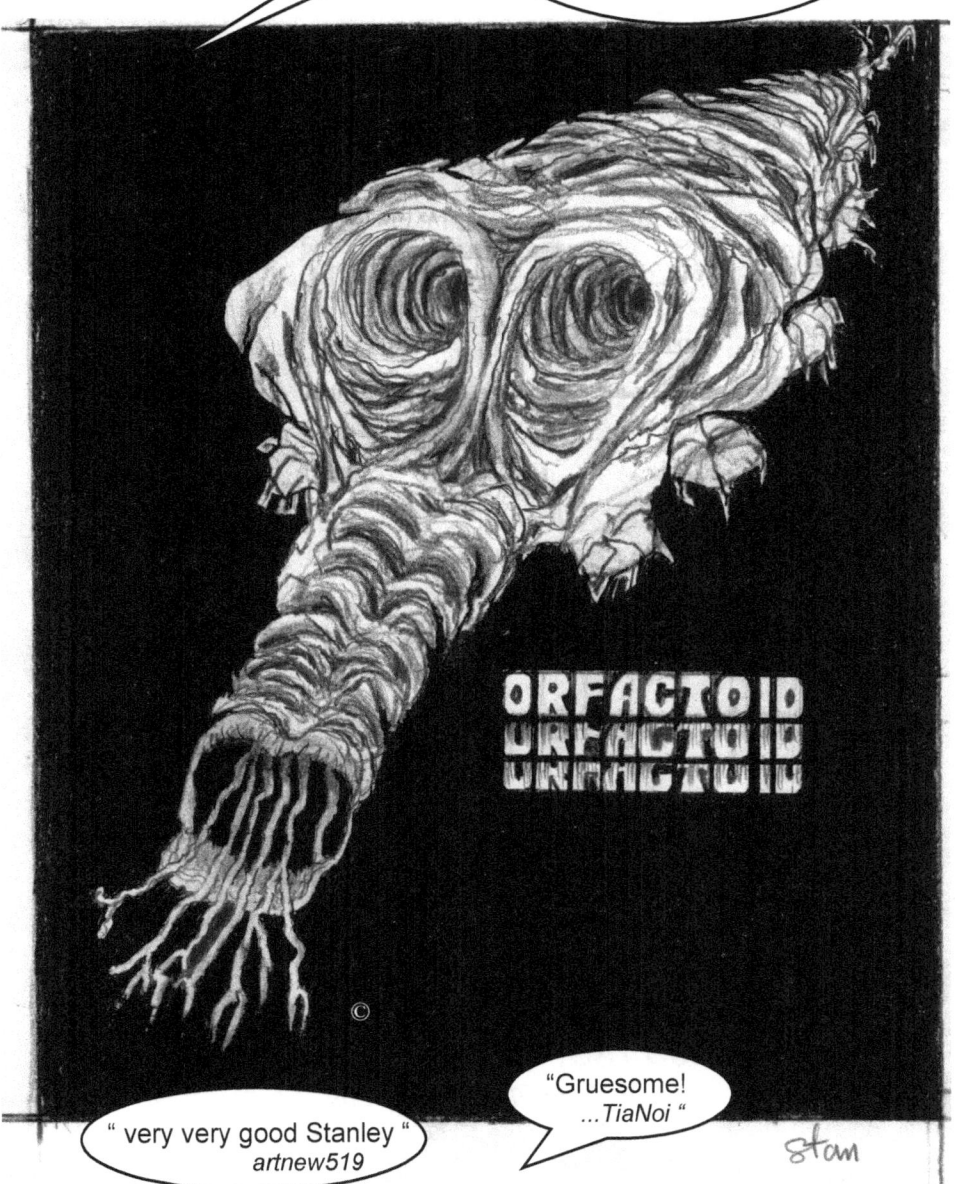

" WELL, PEOPLE WHAT *CAN* I SAY,
ANDROIUS FINALLY LEFT THE CASTLE BUT BEFORE
HEADING UT, HE HAD THE CASTLE-SURGEON
PERFORM A MAJOR BONE GRAFTING AND FACE LIFT
ADJUSTMENTS AFTER SEVERAL HOURS AND
WITH ONE MONTH UNDER WRAPS, THE BANGAGES
WERE FINALLY REMOVED IN FRONT OF THE
KITCHEN STAFF, AND A FEW OF THE GUARDS ..
ALL STOOD MOTIONLESS, FROZEN AND
SPEECHLESS. SINCE THERE WEREN'T ANY
MIRRORS AROUND. ANDY RAN TO THE WATER MOAT
EDGE LOOKED DOWN AT HIS REFLECTION AND
SCREAMED IN HORROR. WELL.. TO MAKE A LONG
STORY SHORT, THAT SURGEON WAS NEVER
SEEN OR HEARD FROM AGAIN.

PUTTING THAT ASIDE. HE'S NOW PROUDLY
SPORTING A BOW TIE AND WITH A PART IN HIS NEW
HAIR. HE FEELS REBORN, READY TO START A
NEW LIFE. HE THEN CHANGES HIS NAME TO ANDY.
HIS LATEST QUEST IS TO FIND HIS TRUE LOVE,
JOSEPHINE, THE YOUNG CHAMBERMAID. WHO LEFT
THE CASTLE A YEAR AGO BUT BEFORE LEAVING THE
CASTLE SHE CHANGED HER NAME TO JOANN .
THEY BOTH PLANNED TO LIVE TOGETHER IN
THE NEW WORLD. THEY WILL BE LOOKING FOR AN
APARTMENT WITH A VIEW OF
THE WATER SUCH AS THE STATUE OF LIBERTY
UNFORTUNATLY THERE IS NO LIVING SPACE
THERE ,SO THEY DECIDED TO HEAD FOR A
FLORIDA SHORELINE
HIGH RISE CONDO.

ANDY

formally

Andrious

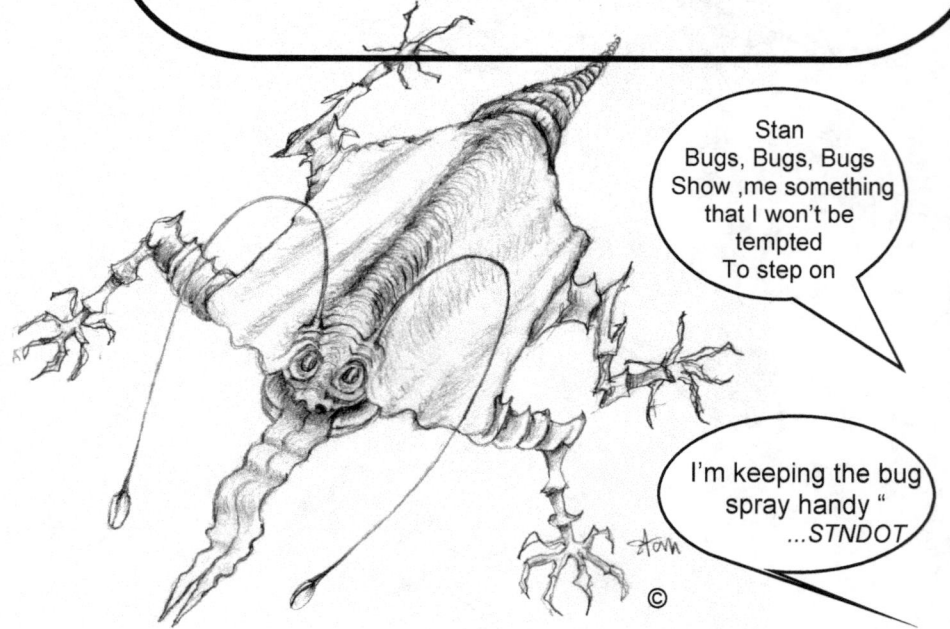

HI PEOPLE, MEET GUY-BUG
ACCORDING TO MY INFORMATION LADY BUGS,
FLUTTERFLYS AND NOW HOPEFULLY "GUY-BUGS", ARE
THE MOST LOVED BY ADULTS AND CHILDREN. THIS BUG
WAS GIVEN TO ME BY ACCIDENT, BECAUSE SINCE
THIS BUG CANNOT FLY, IT SIMPLY ATTACHED
ITSELF TO A PAST ALIEN VISITOR ..THAT ALIEN
VISITOR WAS PLEADING WITH ME " PLEASE TAKE
THIS BUG OFF ME" ..SO NOW I HAVE THE
RESPONSIBILITY TO TRANSPORT IT TO THE
NEAREST FRUIT TREE. THIS "GUY" IS ONLY 3/8
OF AN INCH LONG, NOT INCLUDNG ITS TONGUE, AND
WILL CRAWL TO THE CLOSEST FLOWER BLOOM AND
PERHAPS HE WILL FIND HIS TRUE LADYBUG LOVE. AND
TOGETHER THEY WILL FEAST ON INSECTS .

SS

Stan
Bugs, Bugs, Bugs
Show ,me something
that I won't be
tempted
To step on

I'm keeping the bug
spray handy "
...STNDOT

OK FELLOW ALIEN FANS
MEET VINCENT, A DISTANT COUSIN OF
MORRIS. (I CALL HIM VINCENT BECAUSE HE'S
MISSING ONE EAR)
ANYWAY HE LEFT SUDDENLY LAST NIGHT WITHOUT
SAYING GOODBYE. WHEN HE FIRST ARRIVED, HE
BROUGHT ALONG HIS OWN SACK OF FOOD. I
DID NOTICE THE SACK WAS MOVING INSIDE.
ALIENS DON'T LIKE TO BE WATCHED WHILE EATING.
THE NEXT MORNING AFTER HIS FEEDING,
I DID NOTICE A RED DROP WAS DRAINING
OUT OF HIS FEED TUBE. I HESITATED TO
MENTION THIS TO HIM, I STARTED THINKING.
WHAT DID I GET MYSELF INTO ?
WHEN I SHOWED HIM MY PORTRAIT OF
HIM, HE WAS PLEASED.. I GAVE HIM A COPY AND
HIS GIFT TO ME WAS THE SACK.. IT WAS NOT AS
FULL WHEN HE FIRST ARRIVED EXCEPT FOR
TWO "SEED-EGGS" HE DID TELL ME
SEED-EGG HATCHING DOES NOT NECESSARILY
MEAN SIMILAR LOOKING OFFSPRING ..
THEY WILL ALL HAVE VARIABLE
GENETICS AND DNA. HE DID SAY, IF I WANT TO
ADOPT THEM AS PETS, TAKE ONLY
ONE "SEED-EGG" OUT AT A TIME AND PLACE IT
IN SUNLIGHT FOR ABOUT 6 HOURS AND
THAT I MUST BE PRESENT DURING
HATCHING. IT WILL THEN BOND TO ME

Vincent

"Gruesome! .TiaNoi "
"WOW !, This dude is a slober-er I like it Stan" ....Lily World Dot
"Stan Vincent is a nice looking Guy looks a little Like my brother" ....Frank
"I wouldn't want To be around Vincent. he Frightens me a lot , Ill bet that he is very Quiet most of the time " PuciPaci
SKYSTN @ AOL.COM
©
Stan
"Wewerwererewrwerwerweeeewwwwweeee Slup Slup...part hummer ?" They love that red sugar water we feed em. " ...La Rue Van Gogh

THIS WEIRD FEATHERLESS SKINNY WINGED BUT
FLIGHTLESS BIRD CAME TO ME ORIGINALLY AS A
"SEEDEGG" IN A SACK. IT WAS
GIVEN TO ME FROM THE LAST ALIEN VISITOR AS
A GIFT. I ACCEPTED THE RESPONSIBILITY OF
HATCHING AND FOR ITS
CARING. IMMEDIATELY IT BECAME A FAMILY
HOUSE PEST OR RATHER A GUEST. WE NAMED IT
ZORK AND IT FOLLOWED ME ALL OVER THE HOUSE,
DROPPING IT'S POOP
EVERYWHERE IT WALKED. WHEN IT CAME TO
BEDTIME, NO WAY! NO FOWL IN OUR BED.
A YEAR OR SO LATER ZORK FOUND ITS OWN PET,
A LITTLE MOUSE. ZORK DIDN'T QUITE KNOW
HOW TO KEEP IT, SO HE SWALLOWED IT FOR SAFE
KEEPING. ZORK IMMEDIATLY TURNED BLUE AN
STARTED GAGGING. WE RUSHED HIM TO A
LOCAL VET AND THE LITTLE MOUSE WAS
SAVED JUST IN TIME AND I RELEASED IT IN MY
NEIGHBORS BACK YARD. ZORKS FAVORITE
SPOT WAS ON THE EDGE OF THE BATHTUB
WAITING FOR IT TO BE FILLED .
I TOOK THE HINT AND TRANSPORTED ZORK
UNDERCOVER OF DARKNESS TO A STATE PARKS
WATER SITE. WE SAID OUR GOODBYES.
I DID NOTICE TEARS IN HIS EYES,
BUT I FELT HAPPY KNOWING THAT HE
WOULD SAFELY SPEND HIS DAYS HUNTING FOR
SLIPPERY EASY TO SWALLOW FISH.

ZORK

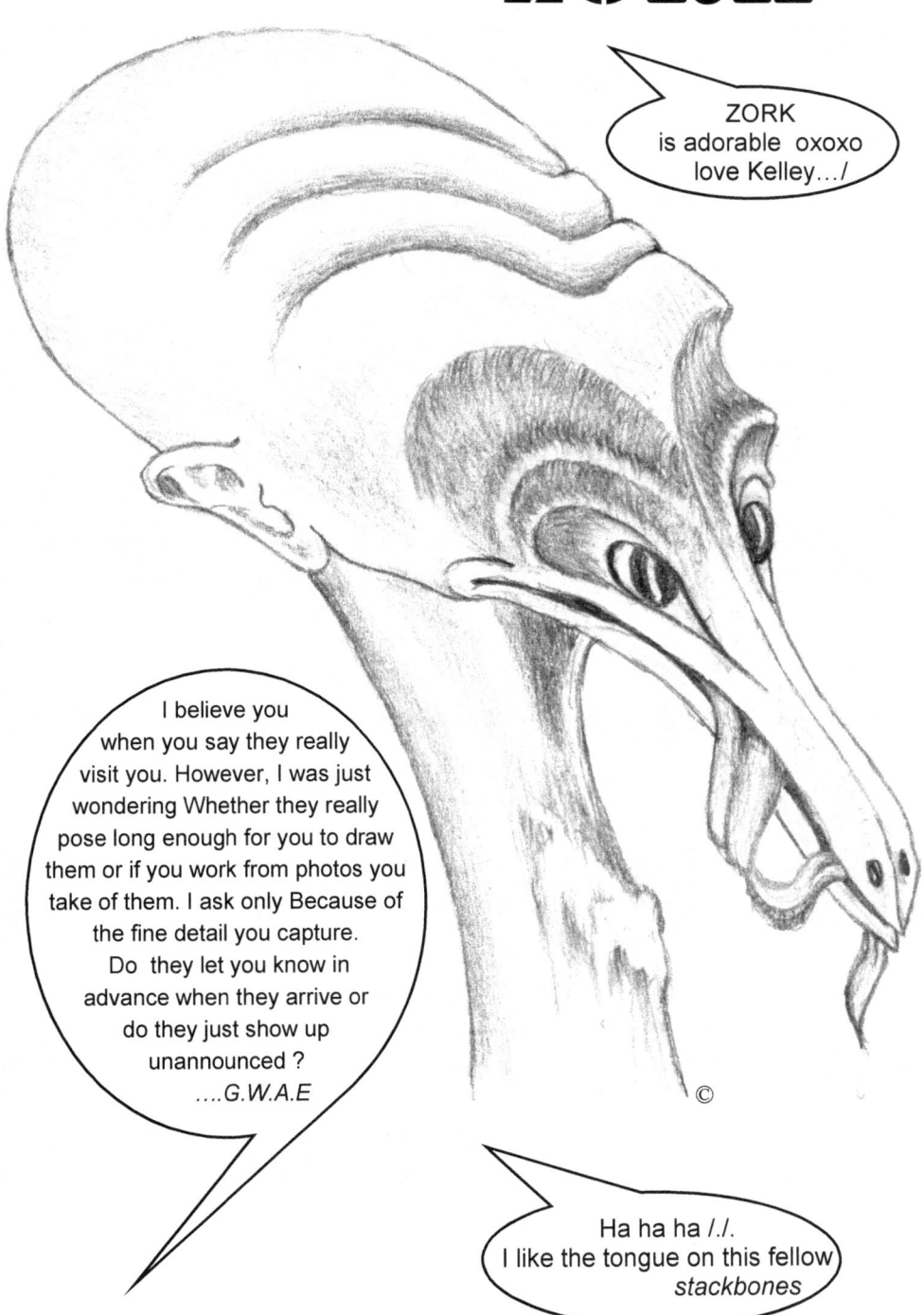

HEY ! GUYS AND GALS
HERE'S MARTHA
A REAL STAY AT HOME KINDA GAL. SHE
MOVES VERY SLOWLY BY SLIDING OVER A
SMOOTH SURFACES. HER HOBBY IS
STARGAZING, FROM THE BEACH
OR ANY SHORELINE THAT'S AVAILABLE
UNTIL DAWN. TO SEEK OUT AN ALMOST
FORGOTTEN WAY-POINT IN THE UNIVERSE
ON HER LEFT FIN SHE BEARS THE FAMOUS
RARE IRIDIUM CRYSTAL FRIENDSHIP RING.
(IT'S AN INTERSTELLA COMMUNICATONS
SENSOR DEVICE)
OH ! BY THE WAY, MARTHA JUST
INFORMED ME, THAT SHE IS HEAVY
WITH "SEED-EGG" AND
SHE'S GOING TO BE AT MY HOUSE WHEN
SHE'S READY TO DROP, WHICH COULD BE
ANY DAY NOW. IN THE MEANTIME, SHE
GOES OFF SHOPPING FOR A SUN HAT.
AGAIN .WHY ME ???

" Oh My Stan
These are all fabulous I love
your Martha You have an
excellent Novella here At best "
.......TiaNoi

"She is heavy with
Egg LOL oh Stan your a crack
up."..

Martha

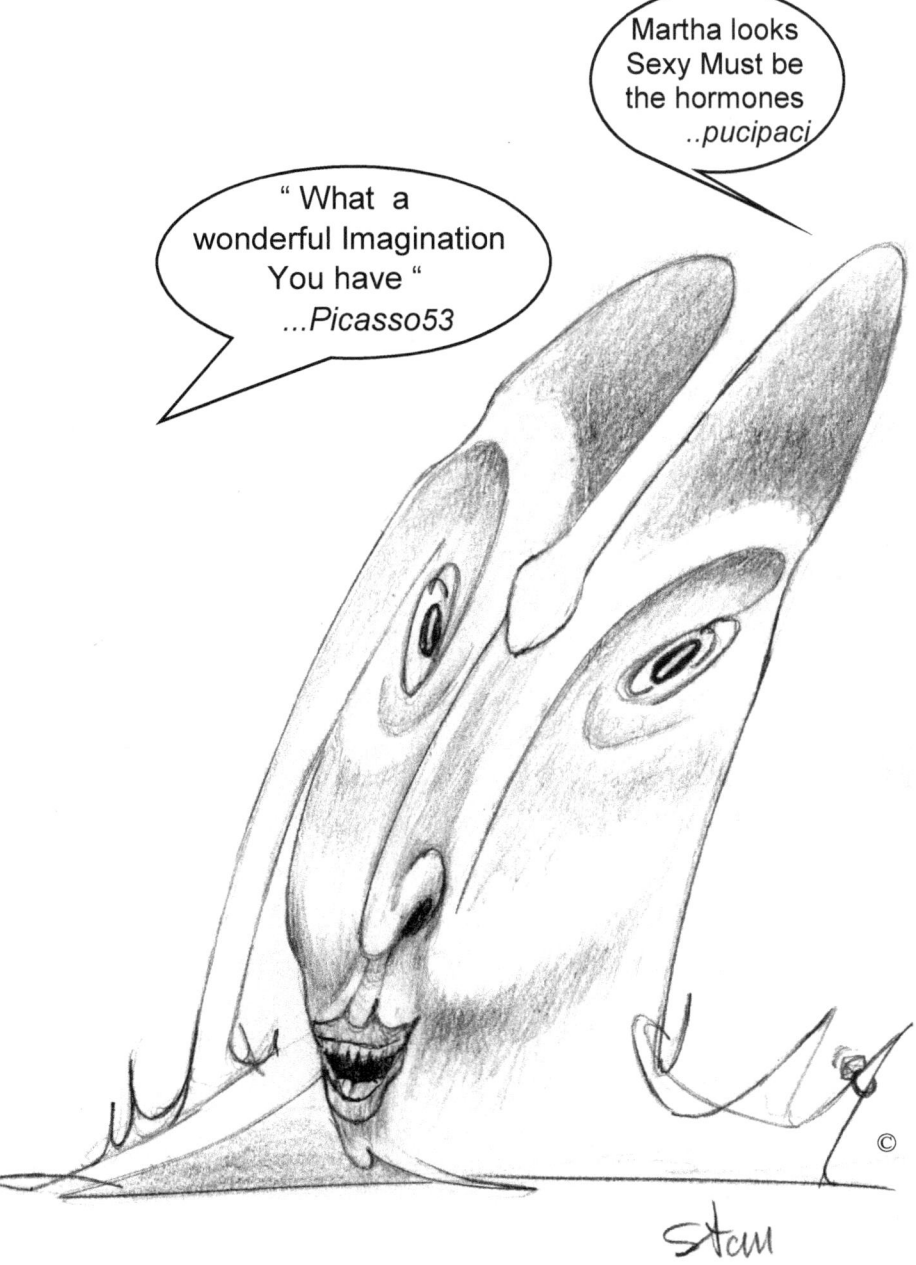

FLASH

SOMETHING WENT TERRIBLY WRONG THIS MORNING AT THE CLONING CENTER AT BUILDING 14, LAB 12B, APPARENTLY CLONE LAB TECHNICIANS STARTED A CLONE PROJECT WITHOUT THE TEAM LEADER BEING PRESENT, WHICH IS AN IMMEDIATE VIOLATION OF RULE 9-1. THE LAB TECHNICIANS THEN TRIED TO HIDE THEIR ERROR BY WRAPPING IT WHILE IT WAS STILL ALIVE, AND CHAINED TO A LABORATORY TABLE, IN HOPES OF DISPOSING OF IT LATER. SOMERHOW IT MANAGED TO ESCAPE AND LEFT THE BUILDING. THE LAB POLICE ARE INVESTIGATING THJOSE WHO ARE RESPONSIBLE AND THEY WILL BE REPLACED. AS OF NOW, WE HAVE THIS ON-GOING PROBLEM. THIS "WRAPPED " CLONED WALKING REJECT. MUST BE FOUND AND TERMINATED... YOU ARE CURRENTLY VIEWING AN ARIST'S DRAWING FROM A DESCRIPTION SUBMITTED TO THE LAB POLICE. NOW, AS WE SPEAK, FOR OUR PROTECTION, A CLONE HUNTER IS BEING CREATED .. OH YES ! A NOTICE JUST CAME OUT... ALL VACATIONS ARE CANCELLED EMERGENCY STAFF MEETING TONIGHT. I HATE WHEN THAT HAPPENS

" He's cool Stan "
Bonlynnart

HI PEOPLE, MEET FRED, HIS PARENTS JUST
DROPPED HIM OFF FOR
THE SCHOOL YEAR BOOK PORTRAIT AND
HE DISLIKES BEING PHOTOGRAPHED.
HE'S 18 AND IS ABOUT READY TO GRADUATE
HIGH SCHOOL. HE'S ALSO
(DNA—GENETICALLY EDUCATED). THIS MEANS
HE HAS ACQUIRED ALL OF
HIS ANCESTOR'S KNOWLEDGE.

THERE HOWEVER REMAINS SOME FINE
POINTS OF HUMAN CULTURE AND
UNDERSTANDING, MISSING IN HIS
EDUCATION. IN THE MEANTIME, HE WILL
BE LOOKING FOR A PART TIME JOB
PREFERABLY IN A PET STORE,
CLOSE TO A FOOD SOURCE. FRED'S FUTURE
AMBITION IS TO SEEK OUT A POLITICAL
CAREER. BEING AWARE OF HIS PHYSICAL
DIFFERENCES HE'S CONFIDENT PEOPLE CAN
LOOK PAST THIS AND JUDGE HIM FOR HIS
GOOD QUALITES

" Stan DNA
Ancestor educated.
I love that concept Fred looks
smart as a whip! "
...MOODMAN99

"Coolness. I think
"DNA instinct ancestor
Educated. Can be referred
to as "Cell memory".
VCBaskermoth

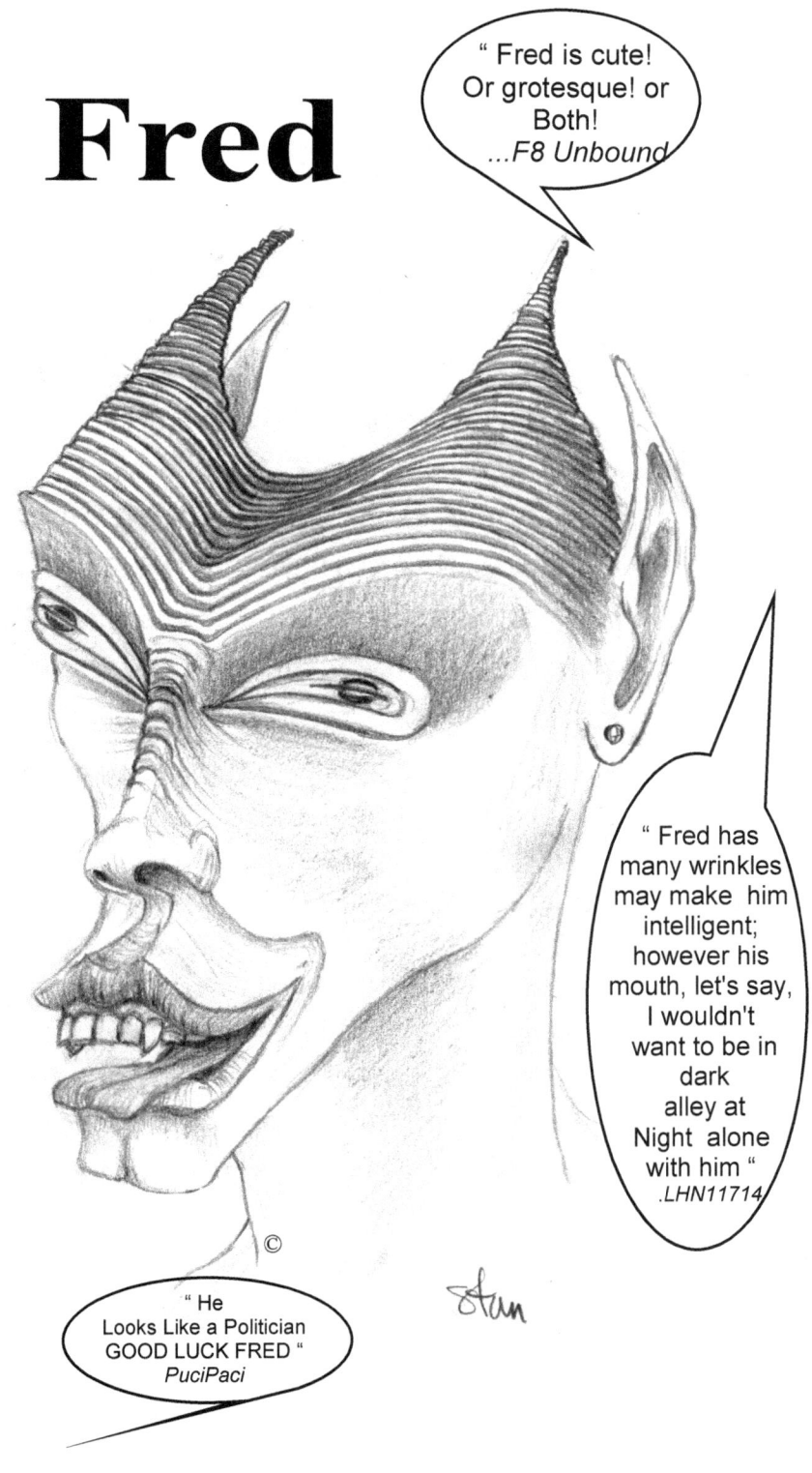

Webtree

IF YOU LOOK CAREFULLY, YOU WILL SEE A RARE AND AN
UNUSUAL SIGHT. A TREE-EYE IN THE PROCESS OF
INSPECTING ONE OF ITS WEB MAKING APPENDAGES TO
MAKE SURE THAT IT IS FUNCTIONING PROPERLY. THIS
CREATURE WAS ORIGINALLY PRESENTED TO ME, ASA GIFT
FROM A PAST ALIEN VISITOR, NOT THE USUAL SEED-EGG
BUT A "STEM-CUTTING" WHICH WILL TAKE A FEW
MONTHS TO GROW FULL SIZE. MY INTEREST IN TREES
STARTED IN MY HIGH SCHOOL DAYS. BASICALLY IT
WAS THE BEAUTY OF THE STRUCTURE HIDDEN BENEATH THE
LEAVES WHICH REALLY INTRIGUED ME, ALLOWING MY
MINDS-EYE TO TAKE OVER MY IMAGINATION, CREATING
WHAT YOU ARE CURRENTY VIEWING. THIS PARTICULAR
SPECIES WILL IN TIME LOSE ITS LEAVES BECAUSE IT
WILL THEN RELY ON CAPTURED INSECTS FOR ITS
NUTRITION. THIS CREATURE HAS THE UNIQUE
ABILITY TO CREATE A WEB SYSTEM FROM ITS INTERNAL
STICKY SAP, THE APPENDAGES PULL OFF THE TRAPPED
INSECTS TO FEED UPON. THESE APPENDAGES ALL WORK
TOGETHER REPAIRING THE WEB WHEN NECESSARY.
BEFORE THE TREE GROWS ANY LARGER, IT WILL
BE TRANSPORTED TO SEEK OUT FOR ITSELF, TO FIND
RICH MOIST SOIL TO SINK ITS ROOTS INTO. IT WILL
THEN ABSORB MOISTERE TO MAINTAIN ITS SAP
PRODUCTION, NEAR A NATURAL LAKE .

Webtree

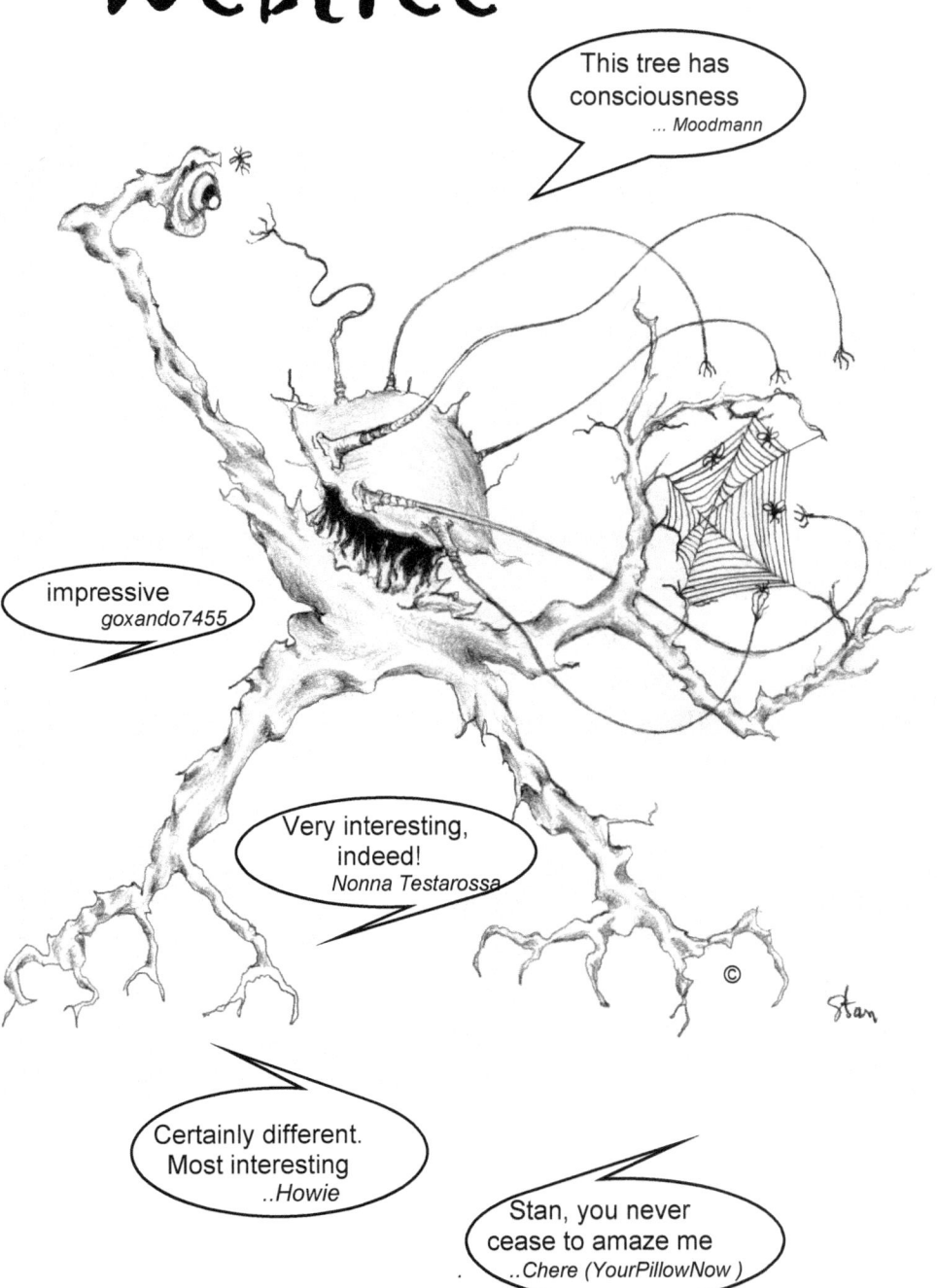

"That's an alien dog if I ever saw one!!! LOL"
...*Picasso50* "

OK "DOG" LOVERS HERE HE IS:
RASCUS
WHO IS ACTUALLY A SYMOVITE..AN ALIEN PUP LEFT
BEHIND MANY THOUSANDS OF YRS. AGO IN THE
HIMALAYAN MOUNTAINS. RASCUS HAS BEEN MASS
PRODUCED AND ALTERED GENETICALLY SO THAT
MANY FAMILIES CAN ENJOY THE
UNIQUENESS OF THIS PUP.. IN THE CLONING PROCESS
ERRORS DO OCCUR.

THE FIRST CLONING CAME OUT WITH 3 HORNS,
A DEFINITE NEGATIVE. SO WE SETTLED ON TWO
SPIKES INSTEAD. WE ALSO DECIDED TO KEEP THE
SPLIT PAWS AS IT'S USEFUL FOR DEFENDING ITSELF
AGAINST MOUNTAIN PREDITORS AND CAN
ACTUALLY STRIKE OUT LIKE A CAT. NOTICE
THE TWO TAILS? THAT IDEA WAS SUGGESTED BY
MY WIFE DOROTHY, CLEVER RIGHT ? NOW TO
ANSWER SOME ON-LINE QUESTIONS; ..LIKE FEEDING
HIM A PARTIALLY OPENED CAN OF FOOD, HE LIKES TO
TEAR THE CAN APART TO GET AT WHAT'S INSIDE. HE'S A
FUN PUP, RESPONDS TO COMMANDS. HE LOVES A LOCAL
POND TO SPLASH AROUND IN AND CHASES SQUIRRELS
FOR FUN ONLY. AT NIGHT HE LIKES TO SLEEP
UNDER YOUR BED AND PROTECT YOU AND IF
YOUR HAND HANGS DOWN
DURING THE NIGHT DON'T WORRY, HE WILL LICK IT.
AND OH YES! HE DOESN'T SHED AND CAN BE
TRAINED TO DO TRICKS.

SORRY I COULDN'T NOTIFY MY FRIENDS
EARLIER BUT, THAT
WAS THE SECOND "SEED-EGG" THAT WAS
PLACED IN THE SACK . YOU REMEMBER , THE
"SEED-EGGS" THAT WERE GIVEN TO ME BY
VINCENT ? WELL, THE SECOND SEED-EGG
HATCHED AND GREW UP. THIS
CREATURE I CALL ZARD, WHO THEN
PROCEEDED TO EAT A CAN OF DOGFOOD
WITHOUT OPENING IT,
..I GUESS HE LOVES THE CRUNCH SOUND.
WELL ZARD
SUGGESTED I DRAW A PORTRAIT OF HIM .. SO
NATURALLY I OBLIGED. HE LIKED IT, ESPECIALLY
WHEN I MADE HIM LOOK YOUNGER. I GAVE
HIM A SIGNED COPY FREE OF CHARGE.
HE WAS HAPPY AND SAID TO ME;
"THOU SHALT HAVE NO OTHER ZARDS
AFTER ME"
I SAID "NO PROBLEM". HE THEN SAID HE WAS
HEADING FOR THE NYC SUBWAYS. HE'S TAKING
THE FIRST FLIGHT OUT ON THE WING OF A
PLANE, AND CARRYING AN EXTRA CAN OF
DOG FOOD WITH HIM.

"Fabulous portrait of Zard!
Remind me not to take a subway in NYC since
I seldom carry a can of dog food in my backpack to
feed the aliens less they ate me"
...puci paci.

ZARD

"Stan... that's 1 ugly dude " ...Frank
"Greatest comeback ever . ..Frank
"Seeing him in the subway would scare the crap outta me ...LOL " ...Dirtypaintbrush
"Do you think Zard will be noticed in NYC?? LOL ….KSpiegel

Say hello to :
Gregg

BUT HIS FRIENDS CALL HIM " MR. G.
" HE'S THE END
RESULT OF A "SEED-EGG" HATCHING
MISHAP, WHICH OCCURRED WHEN HIS EGG
SPIKES DIDN'T FALL OFF.
HE WAS DEPRESSED AT FIRST BUT NOW
UNDERSTANDING HIS PROBLEM,
LEARNING AND ADJUSTING TO MAKE THE
BEST OF IT. HE THEN
REALIZED HE COULD TURN HIS DEFECT
INTO A PERSONAL ADVANTAGE AND
CONSIDERS HIMSELF UNIQUE. ACTUALLY
LUCKY IN A WAY, THAT HIS SPIKES
ARE PERFECTALY SYMMETRICAL.
THAT TO HIM, IS A A DEFINITE SOCIAL
ADVANTAGE. NOW ALL HE HAS TO DO ..IS
TO START A MUSICAL GROUP, MAKE A
MEDIA APPEARANCE AND HE'S ON HIS
WAY TO FAME. ONCE THAT'S
ACCOMPLISHED HE WILL
HAVE PLENTY OF FANS ON BOTH SIDES OF
THE UNIVERSE THAT WILL BE ANXIOUS TO
MEET HIM . ANOTHER IDEA HE HAS.. HE'S
ALSO CONSIDERING BECOMING A HAIR
STYLIST. GREGG FEELS HE HAS A
FLAIR FOR HAIR

OK PEOPLE
MEET THIS GROWN-UP WEED WE CALL

Willie

ORIGINALLY DELIVERED TO ME AS A SEED FROM AN
ALIEN FAMILY VISITORS GIFT. MY
INSTRUCTIONS WERE VERY SPECIFIC.
I WAS TO PLANT IT NEAR A WATER EDGE, 3 INCHES
INTO SOFT EARTH...I DID SO AND WITHIN A SEVER-
ALWEEKS IT SPROUTED AND GREW NO HIGHER THAN
OTHER SURROUNDING TALL GRASSES, AS A
FORM OF CAMOUFLAGE.
HAVING NO MOUTH AND BEING ROOT BOUND WILLIE
WILL FEED ON NUTRIENTS FROM THE EARTH. ,
WILLIE COMMUNICATES TO ME BY CODED EYE MOVE-
MENTS. WILLIE IS HAPPY ABOUT HIS NEW EARTH
HOME AS COMPARED TO HIS LAST PLANET LOCATION.
BEING PLANTED IN FIELDS WITH THOUSANDS OF HIS
OWN SPECIES HE FEELS VERY
INSIGNIFICANT. ALIEN FARMERS ARE VERY CAREFUL
NOT TO HARM THIS UNIQUE WEED CROP,
AS THEY ONLY USE THE OUTER OLDER EDGES OF THE
WEED FOR THEIR FOOD.
WILLIE CAN LIVE UP TO 7-10 YEARS HE WILL THEN
FLOWER GO TO SEED BY SELF-POLLINATION.
HIS SEED GENETICALLY CONTAINS ALL HIS PAST LIFE
MEMORIES. HERE ON EARTH, HE IS HAPPY IN HIS NEW
SURROUNDINGS, WILLIE IS DELIGHTED BY ALL THE
LIVE CREATURES AROUND HIM,
GROUND NESTING BIRDS, BEES AND OF COURSE
DRAGONFLYS AND FLUTTERFLYS.

Willie

"I actually like it ! "
...Brightbabe2003

Intimidating eyes My first thought was a reminder about that old movie. "The Day of the Triffeds"
.....Jean Feathers

HI FANS. WELCOME TARI
HERE SHE'S DISPLAYING HER MOST
SKILLFUL ACTIONS, CLEANING UP FOOD
SPILLS THAT WERE
DROPPED ON THE SCHOOL LUNCHROOM FLOOR.
A VERY DILIGENT PART TIME WORKER.
SHE TAKES NO LUNCH OR COFFEE BREAKS,
DOESN'T SMOKE OR CHATS WITH
THE TEACHERS. SO FAR SHE'S BEEN THERE
ABOUT 2 WEEKS AND THE LUNCHROOM COOK,
BEING SO IMPRESSED WITH HER, IS
OFFERING HER A FULL TIME JOB, SHE
DECLINED. BEING A VACATIONING KINDA
GAL SHE NEEDS TO SPEND TIME VISITING
HER FAVORITE HAUNT.
THE BACK OF A RESTAURANT DUMPSTER.

TARI

HOTDOG EATER

" Hi, skystn poor dogs, lola hug "
.....kipdmud

" Have the people in Coney Island seen him yet? "
....TiaNoi

~even this guy is "Classy" I mean just look at that pinky action!
..LilyWorldDotCom

" Did you know that Nathan's Coney island charging too much for one plain hot dog. Back to the space ship!! I'm outer here
....Hrosenb6

" That's great! Is it a Kosher dog?? "
.....Daniel bi

"lol sky love the new drawing of him eating the hot dog. Thank you for sharing. "
...Karen

" Good Show Stan "
...... Frank

" Ewwww he's drooling all over the place! Lol, someone needs to get him one of those neck napkins to tie around! Quick! Before he floods the place! "
VCBaskermoth

" I LIKE MINE WITH MUSTARD! SERVE ME ONE ANY TIME! "
....Nelj

" Silly Alien.... Dogs are for Cats!!!! Hehehehe Purrr "
.... She8art

" Little Fish, Big Fish"

a Muropodidae-8

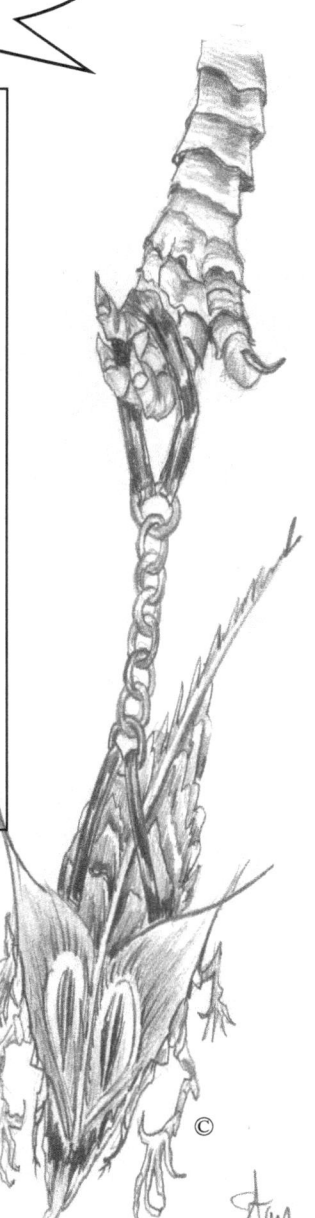

Ok its finally here
A rentable house pest eliminator.
(A cloned and altered DNA)
Muropodidae-8,
shown being delivered by a licensed delivery
agent. This little feller if allowed to roam
your basement at night, by the morning,
all bugs, centipedes, spiders,
large roaches, cave crickets will be gone.
The only requirement, once delivered
into the basement, the door can not
be opened
<u>Unless an official from the company is present</u>
otherwise, they will not be responsible
for what might happen to house occupants
PS.
For some reason the phone company unfairly
refused to issue us a phone number and we
are denied computer accessibility as well.
So we appreciate word of mouth advertising
from already satisfied customers.

WELL FRIENDS HERE SHE IS, WHAT WE ALL HAVE
BEEN WAITING FOR. SHE WAS GIFTED TO ME
AT MY DOOR JUST BEFORE SUNRISE AND AS
BEST AS I CAN SEE, SHE APPEARED AS A CUTE BUT A
VERY HAIRY GAL. THE ALIEN DELIVERY GROUP TOLD ME,
HER NAME IS :

⌘☺▨●♏ ◆⌘◆≋ ❋☺⌘●

BUT ROUGHLY TRANSLATED IT'S,

Gayle with a TAIL

SHE IS ONE OF THE VERY FEW THAT CAME TO
ME, NOT AS A SEED-EGG BUT AS A FULL GROWN
HUMANIZED CREATURE. PROBABLY THE RESULT OF
SOME DNA MIX -UP WITH HER MOTHERS
PAST HUMAN CONTACT. HER ALIEN FRIENDS THEN
TRANSPORTED HER TO MY DOOR AND TOLD HER
THAT, STAN WILL DRAW YOUR PORTRAIT, FIND
YOU EMPLOYMENT AND A PLACE TO LIVE. NOW WITH
THAT TRANSLATED STAGE NAME.. SHE HAS
ALREADY BEEN OFFERED HAIR COMMERCIALS, AS HER
MANAGER ...I'M WAITING FOR A BETTER BUSINESS
CONTACT. SHE JUST HAS TO DISPLAY A BIT
MORE OF HER NECK AND TAIL, AND SHE WILL
LOOK MORE ATTRACTIVE.
MY WIFE IS GETTING CONCERNED.

ANNALISE NEEDS A PORTRAIT DRAWING TO SHOW INTERESTED PEOPLE WHAT A SUCCESSFUL RECONSTRUCTED FACE LOOKS LIKE. SHE ALSO WANTS TO BECOME A MODEL FOR A FASHION MAGAZINE. NOW WHEN IT COMES TO PORTRAITS FOR COMMERCIAL PURPOSES, MY NAME COMES UP, AND THEN SHE SHOWS UP AT MY HOUSE. ANNALISE NEEDS THIS DRAWING TO SEND TO THE "FACE OF THE YEAR BEAUTY CONTEST." ANNALISE HAS NO HAIR ON HER HEAD. AND IS STAYING AT MY HOUSE, SHE IS OUT SHOPPING FOR A WIG SO SHE CAN PIN ON, HERSELF AS WELL AS EARRINGS ALTHOUGH SHE DOESN'T HAVE NORMAL EARS.... FROM WHAT I UNDERSTAND, SINCE THERE'S NO BLOOD CIRCULATION TO HER SCALP, SHE WONT BLEED WHEN THE PINS ARE USED. AS FOR THE REST OF HER FACE, SHE HAS A BROAD WIDE JAW, ENLARGED EYE AND MUMMIFIED TYPE SKIN. I'M PRETTY SURE NO SKIN CREAM CAN HELP HER. AS YOU CAN SEE SHE'S LEARNING HOW TO APPLY LIPSTICK. MY WIFE WANTS HER OUT OF THE HOUSE AS SOON AS POSSIBLE. I CALLED HER FRIEND WHO THEN AGREED TO TAKE HER AWAY.

Annalise...

Dot and Dotty

DUO-HEADED TWINS, A CLONERS
NIGHTMARE.
IT DIDN'T HATCH AT MY HOUSE BUT THEY
DID COME KNOCKING ON MY DOOR WHEN FULLY
GROWN AND WANTED ME TO DRAW THEM. IT
WAS AN UNBELIEVABLE SIGHT.
A TWO HEADED GAL ON ONE BODY THEY WERE
HUNGRY AND WHAT WAS INTERESTING, ONE
LIKES CHICKEN THE OTHER PREFERRES FISH AND
WHEN FINISHED EATING THEY WERE CAREFUL
NOT TO TALK AT THE SAME TIME
IRONICALLY MY WIFE'S NAME IS DOROTHY
BUT I CALL HER DOT. THESE GALS ORIGINALLY
BEING "SEED-EGG" ALIENS, HAVE BUILT- IN
DNA / GENETIC, INTELLIGENCE ..BUT IT ALL
WORKED OUT OK. I WAS GOING TO HAVE THEM STAY
OVERNIGHT BUT THE WIFE SAID "NOOO WAY..
AFTER ALL, IT'S ONLY THE DRAWING THEY
CAME FOR." ANYWAY AFTER DINNER, THEY
SAID GOODBYE AND LEFT TO SOME UNDISCLOSED
LOCATION . I GAVE THEM A SIGNED DRAWING
SUCH AS YOU SEE, AND THEY IN TURN GIFTED ME
WITH A "SEED-EGG" I ONLY HOPE IT HATCHES TO
A NORMAL LOOKING ALIEN.

Presenting

"TERRESTRIS CAPTIS"

MOST PEOPLE HEARD OF THE INFAMOUS VENUS
FLYTRAP, BUT DID YOU KNOW THAT IT'S ALSO
CONSIDERED A CARNIVORE,
THAT JUST WAITS FOR ANY FLYING INSECT TO BE
LURED INTO THE TRAP ?

TO ME, A TRUE CARNIVORE CREATURE, HUNTS....
THIS WAS ORIGINALLY A "SEED-EGG" GIVEN TO
ME AS A
GIFT FROM ONE OF MY PAST ALIEN VISITORS,
TO ACTUALLY HATCH AT MY OWN DISCRETION,
WITH ALIEN INSTRUCTIONS OF COURSE.. IT IS
NOW AS YOU CAN SEE. FULLY DEVELOPED .
THIS HATCHED CREATURE ACTUALLY HUNTS
ITS PREY IN FLIGHT.

>>> EARTHS FLYING INSECT HUNTER A
"TERRESTRIS CAPTIS"

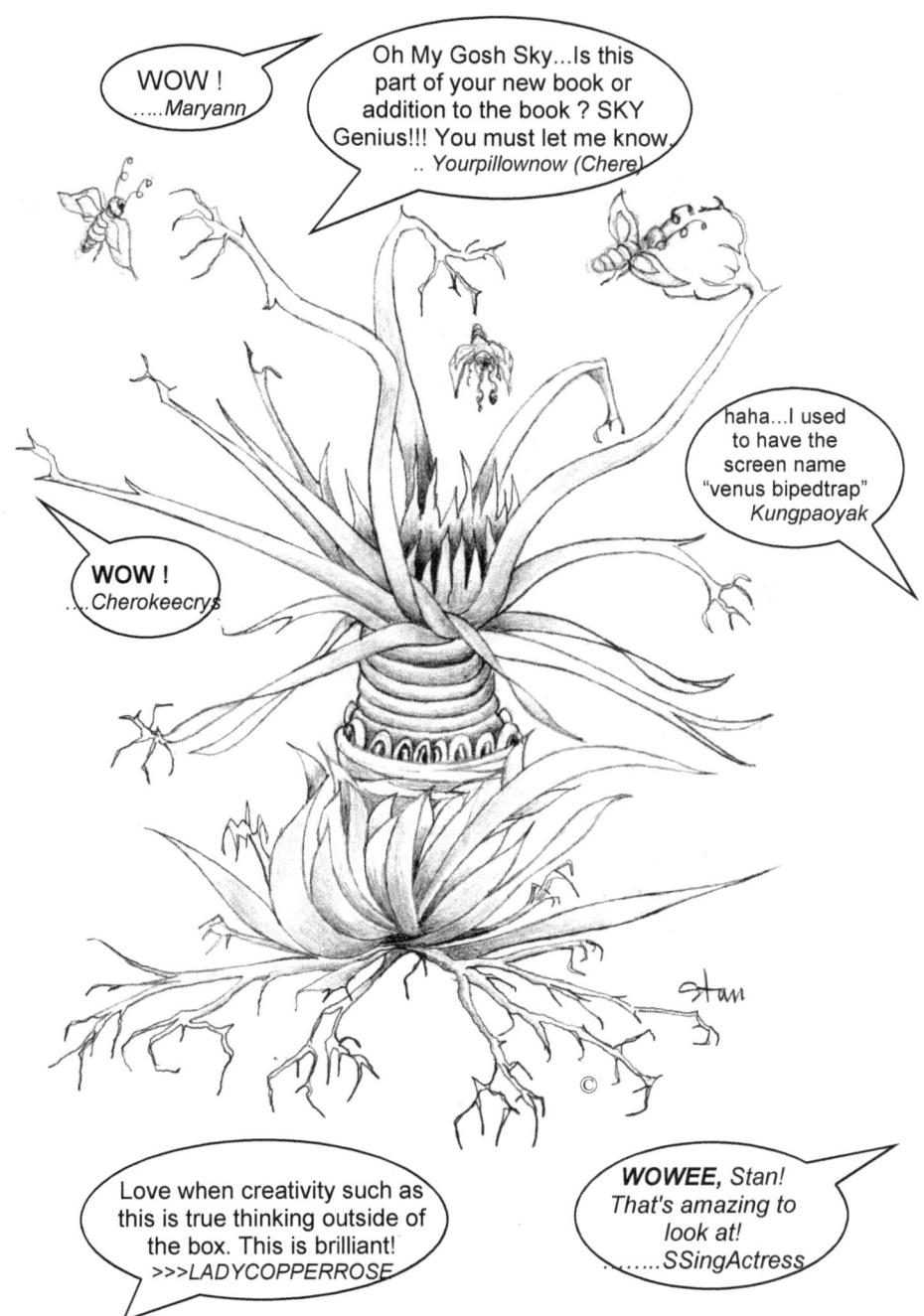

HERE'S PEG THE "PLUNGER"
SHE'S FROM A HATCHING SEED-EGG AND IS
ALMOST FULLY GROWN, IN ALL OF 200 DAYS.
I FORGET WHICH VISITOR LEFT ME THAT ONE.
HER DNA AND GENETICS GIVES HER ALL THE
KNOWEDGE FROM HER ANCESTORS SEA AND
INTERSTELLAR TRAVEL.
ON HER ODD SIDE SHE HAS AN
INFINITY FOR TOILET BOWL WATER,,,
WHEN A TOILET OVERFLOWS , SHE'S RIGHT ON
THE JOB. SHE LIKES THE COOL TOILET
BOWL PLUNGE. THIS IS WHY, IF YOU
NOTICED, SHE HAS NO EARS.
I GUESS THAT'S TO GIVE HER A
SMOOTHER OPERATIONAL FUNCTION.

SHE LOVES PETS AND SHE CAN BE A GREAT
CONVERSATIONALIST AT
THE DINNER TABLE. IN THE EVENINGS
SHE PREFERS TO SLEEP IN A LOCAL SEWER PIPE.
IT'S MUCH COOLER FOR HER.

" My guess is she was
constructed to do her job ....genetic engineered,
so to speak. Perhaps there are no 'males' but the seed-egg
is grown extra-uterus. Good story someplace here.
Perhaps earthlings, too, were constructed and may have run
amok on earth and eventually were given up on."
....mike

" I'd like to place an order for Three please!!! One for every bathroom here Hehehe, Thank you !!! "
She8Art
Peg
The PLUNGER
" She`s another Cutie Stan!! "
moodmann99
SKYSTN@AOL.COM
©
Stan
" PEG has some " personality, let me tell yah "
.... LilyWorldDotCom

OK PEOPLE GUESS WHO WAS KNOCKING ON MY DOOR , EARLY THIS MORNING, ASKING FOR A PORTRAIT DRAWN BY YOURS TRULY,
WITHOUT A CAMERA ? GENERALLY ALIENS DO NOT LIKE ANYTHING AIMED OR POINTED AT THEM. SO NOW LET US WELCOME... MILLIE SHE IS ONE COOL GAL, AND NOW ON EARTH AND WANTS ME TO SUGGEST A PLACE WHERE SHE COULD HAVE HER NAILS FILED AND POLISHED. I MADE THE MISTAKE OF SUGGESTING PERHAPS SOME FACIAL COSMETICS AS WELL, SHE QUICKLY REMARKED BACK TO ME
" I DO NOT WANT ANYTHING
APPLIED TO MY DELICATE FACE TO DISTRACT FROM MY NATURAL BEAUTY AND THEN I WOULD HAVE TO REMOVE IT BEFORE GOING TO BED." MILLIE THEN SAID TO ME,
"SHE BELIEVES THAT FOR MOST
HUMAN GALS BEAUTY IS ONLY SKIN DEEP BUT NOT ME , I'M BEAUTIFUL INSIDE AS WELL. I CAN UNDERSTAND WHEN A PERSON FEELS INFERIOR ABOUT ONES SELF, THERE IS A NEED BUY JEWLERY ADORNMENTS, AS FOR MYSELF, RIBBONS AND LIPSTICK ARE QUITE ENOUGH. MILLIES BIGGEST PROBLEM IS THAT SHE USES UP ALL THE LIPSTICK IN ONE APPLICATION. I THEN SUGGESTED THAT SHE CONTACT ALIZA FOR ADDITIONAL ADVICE, A LONG TIME ALIEN FRIEND OF MINE. SHE TRIED TO CONTACT HER BUT ALIZA'S ALWAYS OUT SHOPPING.

•

MILLIE NEVER TOLD ME WHERE SHE CAME FROM. DOES NOT WANT TO TRAVEL BACK TO THAT "OTHER" PLACE BECAUSE SHE HATES COMPETITON.. ALL THE LADIES THERE LOOK THE SAME.. SHE'S OUT SEARCHING FOR NEW
TERRITORY WHERE SHE CAN STAND OUT AND BE UNIQUE. THIS PLANET EARTH, COULD BE HER IDEAL HOME AWAY FROM HOME. SHE LOVED MY DRAWING OF HER AND THEN BEING AN EGG .LAYER GAL GIFTED ME WITH A SEED-EGG FOR ME TO HATCH ON MY OWN, SHE THEN LEFT .

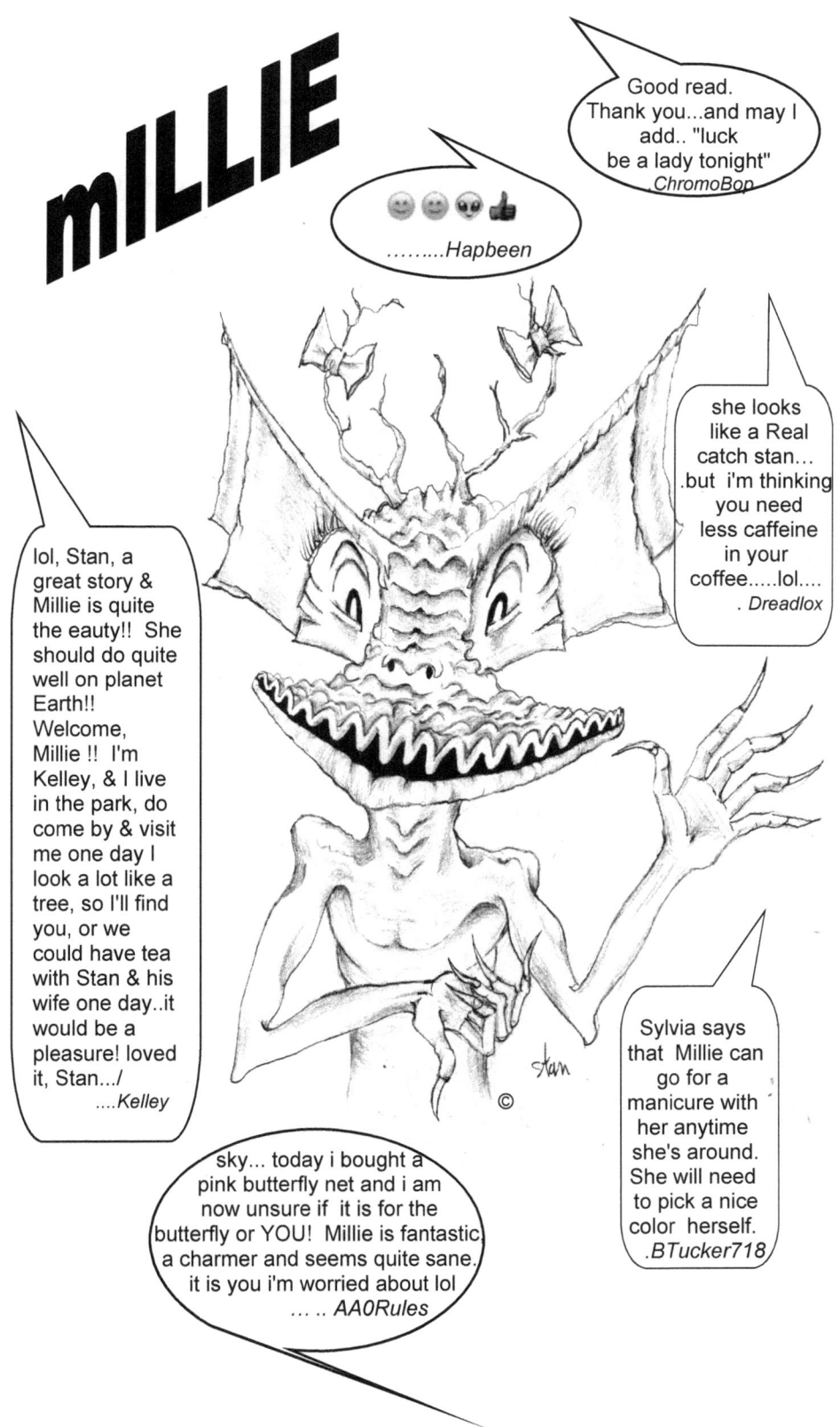

HaVaaN

SOMETIMES WHEN I CREATE FROM MY IMAGINATION WITHOUT A GIFT SEED EGG AS THIS ONE, IT'S A CREATION THAT TAKES ON A MIND AND DIRECTION OF ITS OWN.
THIS HAS NEVER HAPPENED TO ME BEFORE.
IT'S LIKE A CHILD, THAT'S REFUSES TO LISTEN AND SUDDENLY THEY THINK THEY KNOW IT ALL... NOW IT'S CRITIZING OF ALL MY OTHER
CREATIONS, CLAIMING THAT THOSE SEED-EGG HATCHING IS NOT " REAL SCIENCE FICTION.." AND HE IS COMPLAINING " WHY AM I NOT GREEN LIKE ALL THE OTHER HOLLYWOOD GREEN ALIENS, INSTEAD OF THIS BLACK & GREY GRAPHITE CHARACTER IN YOUR BOOK ? COME ON STAN !
MAKE ME GREEN !
THE ONLY OTHER NON-GREEN ALIENS YOU HAVE IN YOUR BOOK THAT I LIKE ARE: MORRIS, MATHEW, FRED, GREGG, VINCENT, MANDY (SHE'S COOL) AND OF COURSE, RASCUS, HE WOULD MAKE A GREAT PET FOR ME I'VE PUT UP WITH YOUR OTHER SO-CALLED
ALIEN CHARACTER IMAGES LONG ENOUGH. I'M GOING TO DISCUSS THIS WITH EINSTEIN AND PERHAPS I WILL TAKE OVER YOUR JOB AS GREETER "

...

I WAS IN SHOCK THAT I, THE CREATOR COULD BE SPOKEN TO SO DISRESPECTFULLY, I THEN REALIZED THAT SINCE I AM THE CREATOR, ALL I HAVE TO DO IS POINT MY PENCIL ERASER IN HIS FACE AND HE SHIVERS IN TOTAL HIMSELF ..I TOLD HIM ONCE HE BECOMES PART OF THE BOOK AND IS NO LONGER LIVING AT HOME, HE WILL THEN BE FREE TO VENTURE OUT ON HIS OWN, GET HIS OWN TV SHOW OR BE A LEADING CHARACTER IN A (SCI-FI) SCIENCE- FICTION MOVIE. EINSTEIN CONTACTED ME AND ASSURED ME WITH A WINK,
I'M STILL THE OFFICIAL ALIEN GREETER.

Flo

OBVIOUSLY FLO CAME A FROM A SEED-EGG, I DID
FORGET WHCH ALIEN GIFTED THIS TO ME. IT HAS
BEEN QUITE AWHILE BEFORE I DECIDED TO ALLOW IT
TO DEVELOP. IT'S A KNOWN FACT THAT A SEED-EGG CAN
BE STORED FOR DECADES. IT WILL START TO
INTERNALLY GROW AS SOON AS THE PROPER LIGHT AND
HEAT CONDTIONS ARE ESTABLISHED. IT TOOK A FEW
WEEKS UNTIL THE SHELLED EMBRYO DEVELOPED AND
BROKE FREE OF THE EGG AND ITS SPIKES, INTO AN ADORABLE
CREATURE. SHE LOVES TO PLAY WIH HER FAVORITE
ALIEN INSECT, JIB,. WHO IS FROM ANOTHER SEED EGG
HATCHING. SHE CLAIMS JIB TICKLES HER TONGUE.
FLO LOVES TO ROAM AROUND IN MY BACK YARD, HUNTING
FOR BELOW GROUND INSECTS; WORMS, GRUBS, ANTS AND
GENTLE AND IS FRIENDS WITH MOST FOUR LEGGED
CREATURES INCLUDING CATS & SQUIRRELS, SHE LOVES TO
RUN WITH OUR DOG BUT OUR NEIGHBORS ARE ANTI-ALIEN.
FLO IS IN THE PROCESS OF CONSTRUCTING A SECRET
"TREE" HOUSE, USING BRANCHES THAT SHE CLEVERLY
BENDS INTO A TOTALLY COVERED HANGING BRANCH
NEST. I PLACED SOME CANVAS FOR HER AT THE BASE OF
THE TREE AND HE USED IT TO LINE THE INSIDE OF
THE NEST POUCH. FLO THEN INVITED ME TO CLIMB UP AND
TAKE A PEEK. I MUST ADMIT IT WAS WELL CONSTRUCTED.
FLO WILL CLIMB DOWN WHEN NONE OF THE
NEIGHBOORS ARE WATCHING. OUR DOG SOMEHOW
KNOWS THIS AND IS LOOKING UP WAITING PATIENTLY
WHILE SHE IS WAGGING HER TAIL.

JUST ABOUT 300 MILLION YEARS AGO SOMETHING
CRAWLED OUT FROM THE PRIMORDIAL SWAMP ON TO
THE SAND , STOOD UPRIGHT, SHOOK ITSELF OFF AND IT
LOOKED UP TO THE SUN AND AT THAT SAME MOMENT
IT'S GOD LOOKED DOWN AND SAID
"ITS NOT EXACTLY IN MY IMAGE, BUT IT IS GOOD "
THE ONLY THING IS, THIS WAS NOT ON EARTH .
EVENTUALLY EARTH ALIENS WILL BRING THIS C
REATURE BACK TO EARTH,
CLAIMING A DISCOVERY. A GREAT FIND FOR
STUDY. MY QUESTION IS, WHO THEN IS THE REAL ALIEN ;
THE HUMAN, OR THE ONE THAT ALLOWED
ITSELF TO BE
TRANSPORTED ? AS FAR AS ITS REPRODUCING
CAPABILITIES, IT DOES SO BY "CASTING OFF" A
PART OF ITSELF. THIS THEN BECOMES AN
INDEPENDENT SUNLIGHT ABSORBING CREATURE AND
IS A TOTALLY MOBILE CARBO—CELLULOUS FIBER ALIEN,
IT WILL MIGRATE OVER ANY PLANETS SURFACE TO
CHANGING LIGHT CONDITIONS. IT IS NOT
PART OF ANY FOOD CHAIN... ACCORDING TO MY
INFORMATION THIS IS NOT THE
ONLY CREATURE THAT WAS CAPTURED BY EARTH ALIENS .
HIS ONE DID MANAGE TO ESCAPE AND OF COURSE FOUND
TS WAY TO MY DOOR. IT THEN ALLOWED ME TO
SKETCH AN IMAGE OF ITSELF. IT
HAS NOW AFTER A FEW WEEKS IN MY BACK YARD,
TRIPLED IN SIZE, BEFORE IT GETS TOO LARGE, I
THEN HAVE TO TRANSPORT IT UNDERCOVER OF
DARKNESS, AND JUST BEFORE SUNRISE TO
A LOCAL STATE PARK ..I THEN WILL RELEASED IT AND
AS IT WALKED AWAY, IT PAUSED FOR A
MOMENT TO LOOK BACK AT ME, IT THEN FADED AWAY
INTO THE EARLY MORNING MIST.

"SkySolSun"

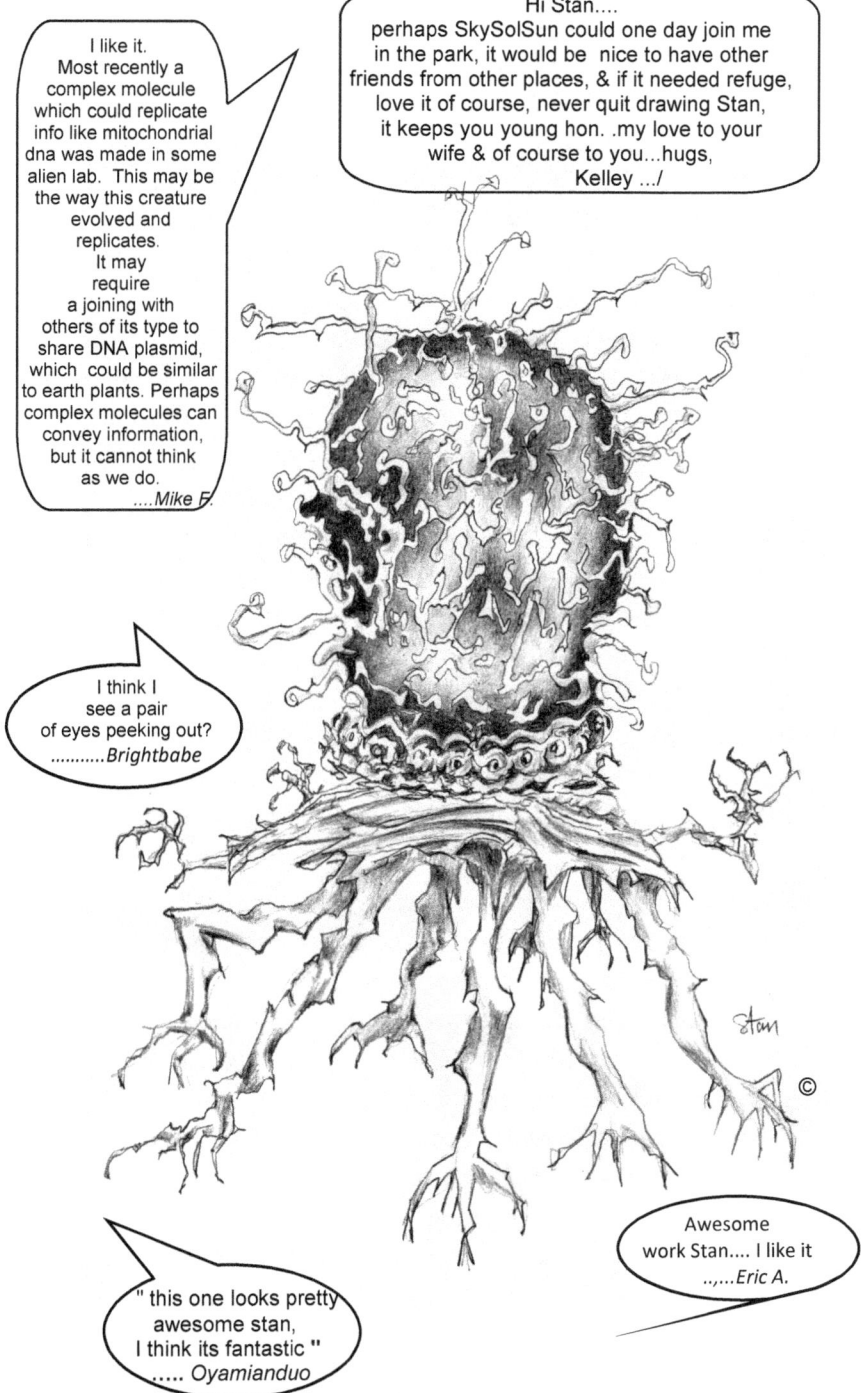

The Branch Brothers

SOMETHING ONE SHOULD NEVER DO IS ... SETTING
SEEDS TOO CLOSE TOGETHER IN THE SOIL..
IT WAS ORIGINALLY GIFTED TO ME NOT AS A
SEEDEGG, BUT AS SEEDS IN A SACK FROM A PAST
ALIEN VISITOR. ONCE GROWN, THEY WILL GROW-UP AND
WILL BOND FOREVER. THEY WILL BECOME A
ONE-FOR-ALL, ALL-FOR-ONE BRANCH BUNCH. THEY WILL
ROAM THE FARMS AND NEIGHBORHOODS TOGETHER, HAVING
FUN SCARING BIRDS AND SQUIRRELS, SCAVENGING
RESTAURANT AND FOOD STORE DUMPSTERS. (THEY LIKE
FOOD THATS JUST A BIT AGED)...AND ALSO WANDER
INTO FARMLANDS AND BOLDY PICK FRUIT RIGHT
FROM ANOTHER TREE AND ANOTHER FAVORITE
SNACK FOOD IS GARDEN VEGGYS, BUT AS DAYLIGHT
APPEARS THEY WILL POSE LIKE PLANTED TREES AND FOOLTHE
UNSUSPECTING PEOPLE WHO WILL JUST
WALK RIGHT PAST THEM .. THE BROTHERS JUST CLOSE
THEIR EYES. REMAIN MOTIONLESS BUT JUST KEEP ON
SMILING...ALL THIS TALK ABOUT TREES REMINDS ME OFAN
UNFORGETABLE AND THE MEMORABLE EXPERIENCE I
HAD WITH A HIGH SCHOOL TEACHER, I HAVE TO TELL YOU.

" While in a high school in a drawing class, The art teacher up front was
instructing the class about perspective drawing ...and
in the meantime I was drawing a tree...(I always loved the tree
without the leaves, to me there is a basic beautiful
structure revealed) ...and as the
teacher was finished, he then did his walk around the
students desks ..when he approached my desk he paused, he
didn't say a word, never got angry, in that I wasn't doing
perspective drawing, he
just sat down next to me and started to discuss how I
could improve the tree I was drawing. A wonderful teacher and
that is something I will always remember about him."

The Branch Brothers

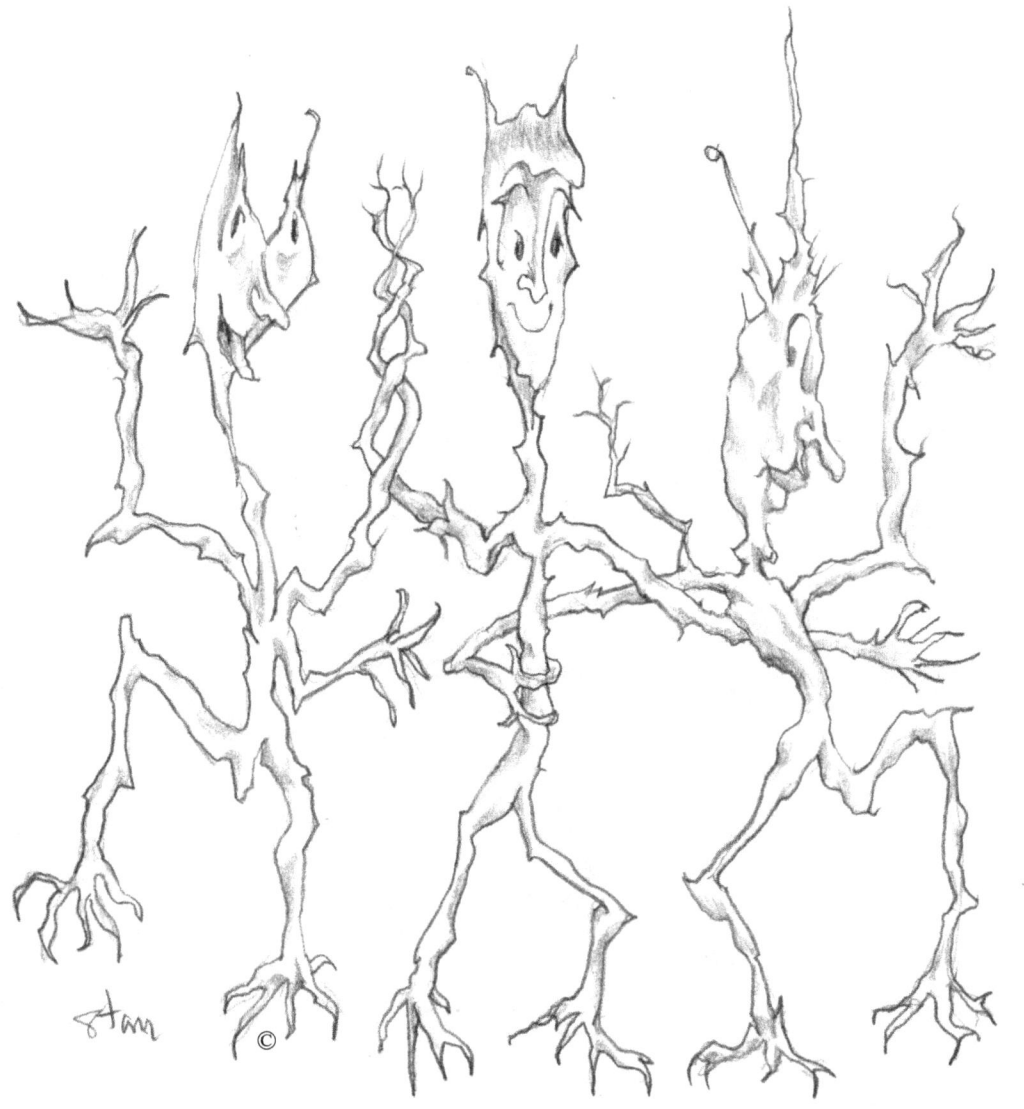

THIS ALIEN GAL WAS DELIBERATELY LEFT
BEHIND ABOUT TWO OR THREE MILLION
YEARS AGO. DON'T BE FOOLED BY HER PRIMAL
APPEARANCE. SHE HAD BEEN
SELECTED TO MATE AND BLEND HER DNA WITH AN
EARLY APE TYPE CREATURE, IN ALL PROBABILITY AN
AUSTRALOPITHECUS.
THE GOAL WAS TO START THE DEVELOPMENT OF
THE HOMO ERECTUS AND THEN FINALLY,
HE HOMO SAPIEN.

PERHAPS YOU MIGHT THINK THAT IT WAS
ALL JUST A DNA MUTATION, HOWEVER, THE
FACT IS THAT ALIENS DECIDED THAT CONQUERING
EARTH BY CREATING WARS AND DEVASTATION
AND DESTROYING THE HUMAN RACE, WAS NOT THE
BEST WAY
FOR ALIEN SURVIVAL.
IT WAS THEREFORE EASIER FOR ALIENS TO
BECOME PART OF AND TO BLEND IN WITH
HUMANKIND, THEREBY ALLOWING THE
EVOLUTION TO GO FORWARD. CONSEQUENTLY, WE
BECAME THEM AND THEY BECAME US.

I HOPE THAT ONE DAY, SOME FORENSIC
ANTHROPOLOGIST WILL
DISCOVER HER BONES AND NAME HER...

I love her
choice of earrings
.....Spk2me117

Neila

...AS I DID

Looks great. I love her
earrings. From her
expression, it looks like She
likes it, A gift from her mate
no doubt. "
.......,,,Jeanfeathers

She looks like a sweetheart,
ready to mate
.........lhn11714

I JUST CAME BACK FROM A DEEP SPACE
EXPLORATION, AND IT WAS A PRIVILEGE TO
BE ON BOARD. THE CREW'S PLAN WAS TO
SEEK AND FIND A METEOR THAT WAS COMING
CLOSE ENOUGH TO EARTH AND PLACE A
TRACKING SENSOR ON IT.
IN OUR LASTEST DESIGNED
" CLASS G " QUA-MOBILE SPACE-UNIT. "
EVERYTHING WAS GOING ACCORDING TO
PLAN UNTIL, WE DID ,ENDEED ENCOUNTED A
RARE SIGHT. TWO BIO'S IN A CONFRONTATION,
APPARENTLY
ONE OF THE DEFENSE BIO UNITS MISTAKENLY
ATTACKED A FRIENDLY RATOM.
FORTUNATELY IT CEASED IT'S ATTACK IN
TIME AND MOVED AWAY. WE DID MANAGE TO
IMAGE RECORD THE INCIDENT.

THIS WILL APPEAR IN THE LATEST ALIEN
UNDERGROUND NEWSLETTER.
EARTHLINGS NEED NOT BE CONCERNED
THEMSELVES. THAT BIO CRAFT WASA DEEP SPACE
HUNTER, PROGRAMMED ONLY TO SEEK OUT AND
DETER UNFRIENDLY BIO-IRIDUM SPACECRAFTS.

" The drawing I saw today my favorite
by far. The two eyes looking at each other
It was "seriously" cool! "
...LESAMONET.

Confrontation:

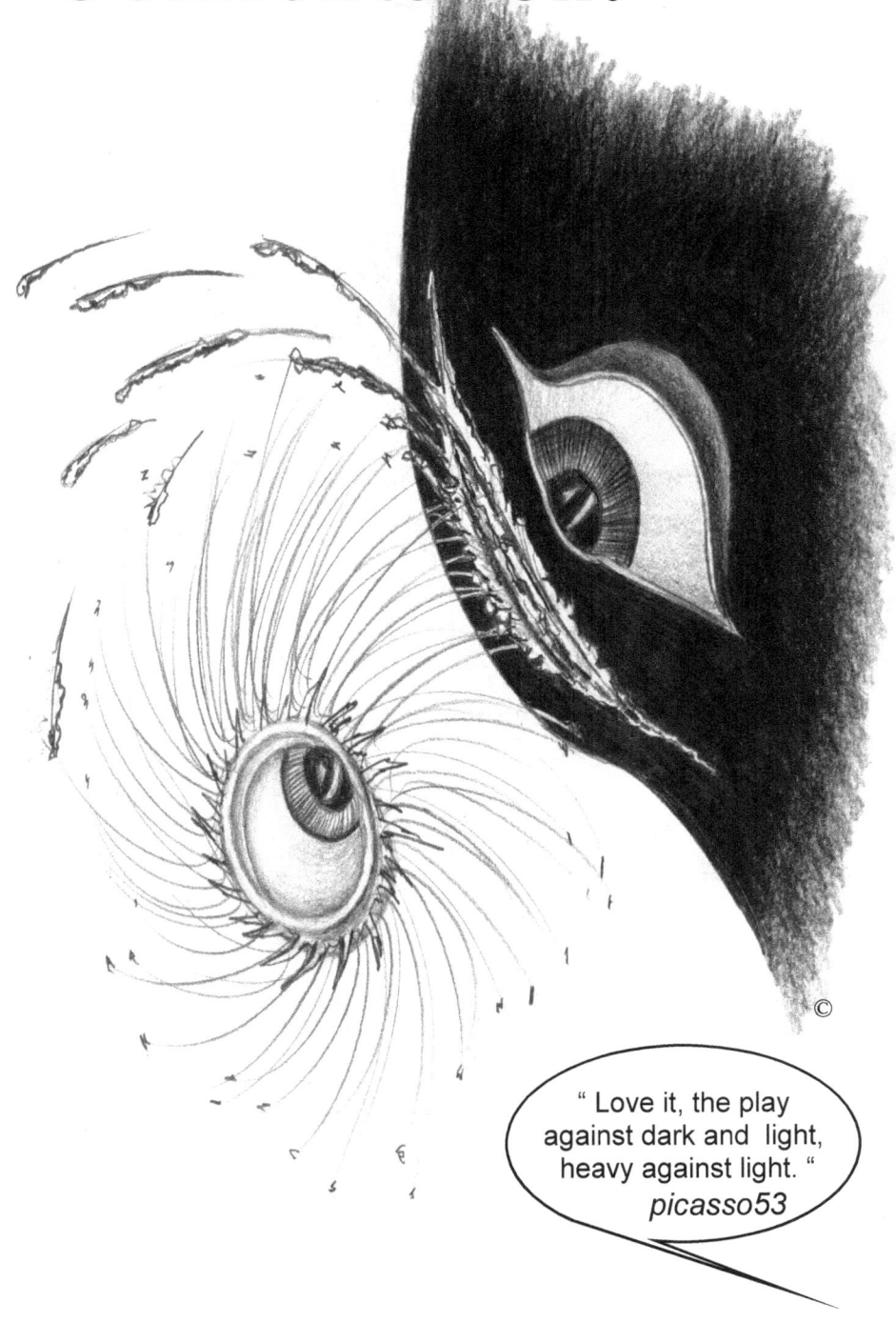

" Love it, the play against dark and light, heavy against light. "
picasso53

Well people ....The ultimate did happen...

You wouldn't believe who visited me, it was

the Chairman of all future aliens :

ALI-EiNstein ©

I received a carbo-metalla eyescan sheet announcing

his visit and that I was required to maintain

secrecy about his arrival..

During our meeting ...

He stated : Because I was so protective and caring
to all " Seed-Eggs "

He honored me with an:

Official Alien Membership

" relatively speaking." he left that evening

ALI-EiNstein

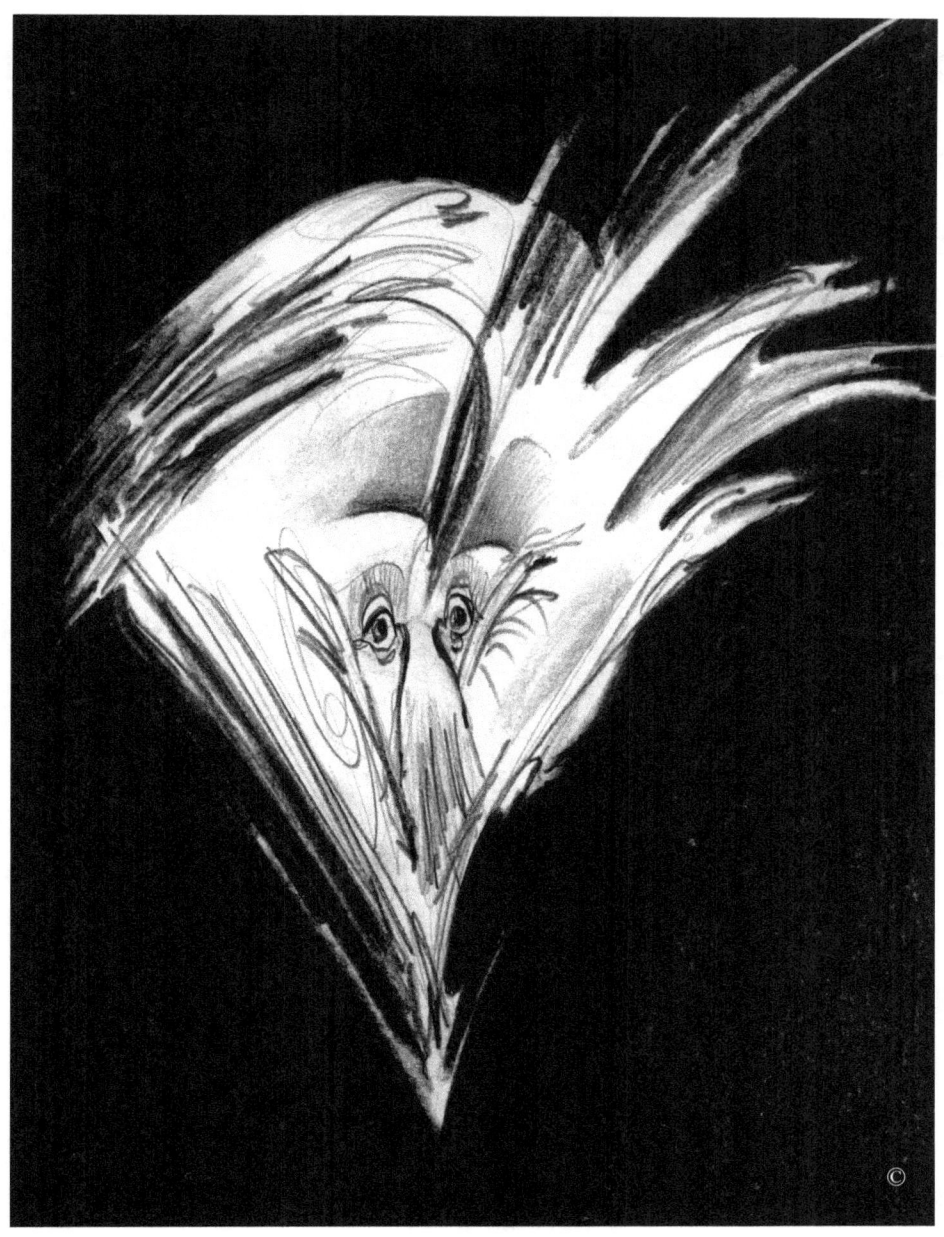

Hi
I'm trying to track down how all this began for me,
from my many of my primal drawings.
The one shown here, was one of many in my
collection, that allowed my
evolve, into the
ALIEN SCENAIRIO
So in hindsight ...I will call this one
"Alien *Landscape 1 "
Your comments are welcome ....stan

" Reminds me of those movie scenes
where they show the floor, and then someone
opens the door and the light floods through but you can
see the shadow of the person standing in the doorway.
The floor (even though I know its not really) looks
like it would be rippled like foil or something. Cool "
VC Baskermoth

" OOOO this looks like a
deadly weapon of sorts!!!!!!! it looks like
some sort of Blade I'll take two for my Boyz for
Xmas hehe '
... *she8art*

Alien* landscape 1

My education in art started with J.H.S., High School and continued on to college. I eventually became a graphic artist working for various companies. I was then employed as an illustrator for the New York Department of City Planning. After a time I advanced to Art Director.

During that time and into retirement, I was drawing, and painting on my own The idea for this book "Alien Visitors" came much later. My first alien drawings came on very gradually. It began as a fun thing ... I drew Morris first and let the background image become his girl friend and I named her " Mandy " and then, it took on a life of its own.

WELL, THE STORY BEGINS LIKE THIS :
It all started around 2009 when aliens would visit me. It is a well-known fact that aliens are actually afraid of cameras or anything that's pointed or aimed them, they would rather sit or a drawing. (what a great opportunity for me)
When completed, they would present to me a gift, which I call a " seed-egg." A seed can last for many years before germinating, an egg cannot, but combined, it can last for decades.

....Another interesting thing is that hatched alien "seed-eggs" do not have to look like the parents. This is because Genetics and DNA are variable. What is most important is that every alien respects and cares for all seed-eggs no matter who lays it, so therefore they have >> " Universal Care." .....

Each alien that visits me has their own personal agenda for coming here.

Although I never ask, some do tell me. For example, one visitor left and wants to spend its days in the back of a restaurant dumpster, with an ongoing food supply.

Another wants to be transported to any house with large TV Screen or to a Movie theater to spend its days eating floor-dropped popcorn.

I hope you enjoy this book with as much fun as I had in creating it .

......Thank you   ...stan

This book is dedicated to all of my online friends, and relatives, whose suggestions and criticisms helped me create this book and to my wife Dorothy and my Daughter Brenda Santoro, my production advisor.

For more information about myself or my art, I can be reached via E-mail as : SKYSTN@aol.com .... or Stan Shabronsky on the internet or "GOOGLE" SKYSTN6148@Gmail.com